Guilt, Shame and Poverty: Love, Loss, Betrayal

A Collection of Short Stories

I0633680

Shane Leah

chipmunkapublishing
the mental health publisher

All rights reserved, no part of this publication may be reproduced by any means, electronic, mechanical photocopying, documentary, film or in any other format without prior written permission of the publisher.

Published by
Chipmunkapublishing
PO Box 6872
Brentwood
Essex CM13 1ZT
United Kingdom

http://www.chipmunkapublishing.com

Copyright © Shane Leah 2011

Edited by Aleks Lech

Chipmunkapublishing gratefully acknowledge the support of Arts Council England.

Author Biography

I was born into the Klosowski/Leah family on the 2nd of April 1980, at 10.17 am, a Tuesday I am lead to believe at the Countess of Chester Hospital. My father worked for the local Council in the Highways Department and my mother was a married mother of one son already; my older brother Darryl. We grew up in a stable and loving home during the 'golden age' of the Thatcher years of government; hard work and piecemeal rewards are what my parents' remember of their early married lives. But we were very happy. My parents went on to have another 2 children other than me and my older brother before my they divorced and then my mother had a fifth child by her boyfriend. My older brother and my eldest sister have families of their own, whereas my little brother is in the Middle East teaching adrenaline sports, rock climbing, scuba diving and the like. My littlest sister is the star of the family; we are all very close.

My diagnosis with a mental illness came in the late autumn or winter of the millennium period after a series of crisis within my family and my relationship with my then, girlfriend - Dawn. Around Christmas time I had a breakdown over my concerns for the future of my relationship with my said girlfriend and my family chose to call a doctor to deal with my verbal aggressiveness and erratic behaviour. It is true I had spent the run up to the millennium getting out of it on whatever drugs I could get my hands on. Several weeks had passed like this and I was talking gibberish and hallucinating that my fears would get the better of me... Needless to say they certainly did, but many years had passed before I realised the extent of my errors and by now it all pales into the past. I guess you live and learn, but you must get to grips with whatever triggers the psychosis and hostility if you are to survive schizophrenia.

I am grateful to the work of the many psychiatrists who have supported me over the years and allowed me enough time and understanding to get back to the way of life I had before my drug problems and subsequent breakdown. Without their help, I may never have survived my twenties and would have left a massive black hole in many of the lives of those that do love me.

My interests include mellow guitar music such as The Beautiful South, Damien Rice, Mercury Rev and Nick Cave and the Bad Seeds, amongst others. I am also studying towards a BA in Literature with the Open University, when I am not writing autobiographically of my experiences of schizophrenia. I also offer advice to others suffering with, or caring for people with mental health issues on the internet, through weblogs or other internet sites. And I am a big fan of horoscopes!

I am also just graduated this year (2010) with a Diploma in Literature and Creative Writing, DipLCW(open), with the Open University.

If you would like to read more on my experience of schizophrenia, the world we inhabit and the tabloid press, then please visit my blog at;

www.deadcitystreets.com

Here you will find regular updates of my thoughts on what occurs around me as I transverse life and all its boundaries, from within the mind of a passionate and obscured, observer.

And if you like this novel and would like to know more about my experience, I have one other short autobiographical novel called Dead City Streets, also available from Chipmunka Publishing.

Shane Leah

Prologue

As a child, I had a conversation with my aunt about the history of our family. I was trying to trace my family tree and so I asked about my grandparents and I told her what I remembered of my grandfather, Bill Dutton. She must have had a real big problem with the issue of our genealogy as she told me on no uncertain terms that Bill was not her natural father. No, she and her siblings had a different father, who rather than being the war hero I had expected to hear about, was a Nazi war criminal.

I only had memories of Bill and fond memories at that.

So who was Victor?

Victor, it would seem was some sort of beast, an evil fascist. The story Barb taught me while still sat upon her stool had been handed down to all of the family at a particular age, 14. I had not expected to hear such a horror story of grotesque abuse in all my life except on the silver screen at home when I sometimes woke in the early morning because some unknown, creeping, image of a ghost had woken me from my sleep. Puberty in my particular family was seen as some dark, dirty thought that you ought to rub the babes' noses in or to wash their mouths out with carbolic soap.

Yes, I was rocked to the core by the allegations my aunt whipped me with, saying her father was a child abuser and so as a matter of consequence and genealogy, I too was to become the most frightening thing I have ever been accused of being. I didn't understand? But then again I professed I did and would take her word as the gospel to avoid ever becoming the devil she described that day.

For the rest of my life the legacy of Victor was always watching me, tapping me on the shoulder and making me fearful of ever being caught with my trousers down. Always reminding me of why my parents were divorced – because when I was 12 and my sister was 6, she was raped by a neighbour and the family fell apart. The curse of the family had struck its first blow to us, a young family trying to live, learn and make love. The spectre of Victor was born unto us.

I have never gotten over it. To this day I still feel as though I have something to apologise for because I am fearful of my base feelings and drives. I have been shown some ugly emotions as I grew into an adult but none compare to my own feelings of inadequacy, fear and hatred that I dredge up from the depths of my being whenever I reach inside for answers to the questions people demand of me.

And the demands are to fuck, lie and get wasted.

A psychic I called early in my thirties asked me 'who do the following 4 words remind you of?'

'Jealousy, fear, frustration, sexuality.'

I answered piously that the words were my very living malady. After all, I was a failure in human relations, assertion, work and sex as a schizophrenic. I had seen none of these things fruit for me in ten years. And really, I had no idea why I was so inept?

In previous years I had been battling with friends over the very ideals I held in my heart for the one I was seeking. One particular group of 'friends' had hurt my feelings many times before as they demanded I succumb to their way of living their lives. According to gospel of my friends,' I was to get a job, pay my own rent, to give generously of all I have, smoke shit and listen to their false teachings on how to treat women; with contempt and hatred.

Yeah. Fuck, lie about it and get wasted.

I wasn't interested in what they had to say. I had dreams by then of how my life could be and I had taken it upon myself to fight for my right to be respected as a human being and allow my feelings to show, to be heard and to be recognised! And that is why I have spent my life being beaten to a pulp...

Even as a younger adult, I was criticised to the utmost by the friends I had made to 'up my game,' to respect my elders and to keep quiet about the more aggressive and abusive memories I remembered when I was psychotic. And I did but as I grew apart from these friends in my twenties I grew more suspicious that something was very wrong in my family and friendships. No matter how they treated me, I would not tell until my psychiatrist asked the obvious question.

'What's up at home.'

'Everything.'

From the legacy of Victor's passing to the current attitude of my family members; the seeds of something black, with evil intent was lurking within the whole family dynamic. I didn't want to understand but nor could I seriously run away. The 'voices' would find me and they would kill me.

So, no! I do not understand why Victor was the beast he

grew to be and I would not want him to be the dark thought that catches me someday making love and judges me according to the word that makes my head hurt and my ears ring. No, I am afraid the living are all too full of their own greed and lust for me to fear the dead. The beast that is the living have already left to find human flesh…

So, what about me, I may ask?

Well, all the patience in the world has not rewarded me as I would have hoped. No woman in my life is 'with child' and it is looking doubtful whether I will ever prove myself as a parent.

But why is it this way?

And how am I ever supposed to survive this transition?

My Affairs of the Heart

In my search to be loved by another, I have suffered many indignities and been enslaved to the passions and whims of people I was entirely dependent on for emotional sustenance. I have been used and abused and what is more, I still am hostage to the expectations of those that surround me. In their estimation, I am suffering from loneliness and neglect of my heart. It is true then, that when I say that I am unloved, you can be certain it is true. Otherwise, might I not say that I feel it in my heart and soul?

Of course, I have the same desires and fantasies as a regular human being but suffer from the terrible affliction of always suspecting we are merely mammals acting out social roles that fulfil us. I half suspect it is true, nevertheless.

The only counter to this malaise of suspicious and paranoid thought, are my suspicious and paranoid thoughts, that witter on to me daily, just as soon as evening arrives or I partake in the smoking of cannabis. These incessant whispers that ruminate on the present conditions of my own malaise to be unloved and unwanted often go in ever decreasing circles as I make a discourse with the disembodied figures of people I know but who are not present with me, at that time.

I guess the symptoms I have just described are crucial and constant to the diagnosis I have been given of Schizophrenia. It is not an illness you would like to be suffering from. Just several years ago when my dreams were at their most lucid, I often found my nocturnal habits would interfere with my waking life. Many times I would settle off to sleep after a lengthy pillow talk with my own alter ego, only to be woken 20 minutes later by my own screaming voice. An insane rage of obscenities would flow from between my own clenched teeth and I would flail my arms around as if hitting or stabbing some invisible demon. Often those demons were those I loved the most, my father, mother, friends and girls I hoped to fall in love with some day. Pity me, because my heart was so deep and so full with the iniquities of a greedy society that sought to replace me, I had no greater love than that of myself. Alone I shall be, and for evermore. That was the question.

And worst, temper of my own demise, it was my desire to love as I dreamed that brought me here. I really, really wanted to believe in the feelings I had in my heart for those I loved, but always I had doubts. And when I was certain? Well, I never was that certain I did have feelings, and much less doubt I ever did love anyone, as others took for granted. Ashamed I may be of my nocturnal desires, but I did believe love would find me one day and then I would know.

The problem as I could see it at 28 years of age, was that life and those I lived it with had taught me some dear and to be true, some wrong lessons. A few things in my life just didn't stack up. My loneliness just for starters; I seemed to be hated by all and sundry in the town in which I lived. I was reckoned, I believed, to be some kind of beast, an object of derision and scorn. Many thought me to be a paedophile, which was never easy on my conscience as my mind was already tortured with guilt and shame. Much the same could be said for my subconscious belief that I had allegedly raped a girl several years earlier on a drunken night out, and was probably a trigger to the hostile chants I would often shout out loud at the four walls of the flat I inhabited during this period. It was a terrible curse to live under.

Even in my dreams when asleep at night, images of children would enter my mind as I wandered from dreamscape to dreamscape by means of canals, winding lanes and railway tracks; always terminating in a sexual encounter, before waking in my bed with a feeling of guilt and shame. Before long, these erotic fantasies began adversely affecting my waking life. I became sallow in public and especially around children. I would have sleepless nights worrying about the shame of getting caught with my trousers down and yet I could not beat the beast. I was under the control of a force so great it demanded the best of me and discarded the doubts that had plagued my mind for so long. It seemed, I thought, I was in love. At last! Was this the Holy Grail I had searched so long for? My behaviour was criminal and my psychiatrist eventually saw the truth. I was afraid of being unloved.

My whole life I had suspected something was wrong with me. As a child I often felt lonely and would complain to my parents that other children on the estate where I lived would not play with me. I really needed that dearest, closest bond with one other human being other than my own self. And I did eventually find one in my earliest friendship with a boy across the road from where I lived, called Steven Waters; later to be replaced by the affections of my mother.

An Oedipus relationship blossomed between me and my mother at the age of 11, as soon as I started to become interested in girls, particularly in magazines. I believed myself to be my mother's saviour. Her darling little boy would do anything to please. Soon she began to take direction in my life, ordering me to sleep with her choice of partner and flattering my fledgling ego with gushes of pride in my intelligence. I was a good boy and I never wanted to be anything else. Soon we changed address to a bigger house to contain our ever growing family of now 5 children and a dog. Already, something was up with my young mind and my mother would sometimes ask odd questions about what I was doing late at night. I never had any recollection of my strange acts of defiance in and around the house as I grew to be a teenager, but the evidence came soon after my 13th birthday, when I began acting erratically.

What makes this time stand out is a friendship I had made with an older boy called Simeon. I recall how I met him. I was having trouble at school, I wasn't liked very much and was constantly harassed by other more socially able kids in my school when they went through the key stage 3 development; sex education. Fact remains, I didn't get to indulge myself in the practical side of the bargain. And my course to isolation and regret was sewn into the fabric of my unconsciousness from that day forward. I felt a failure, unwanted, unloved and most of all humiliated by myself and my body for want of just a kind word and a little help. Just a friendly face.

I got the help, all right, soon after. My brother arranged for me to meet a girl who lived nearby called Kim, and we struck up a brief, clandestine relationship, to my greatest pleasure and glee. Or at least that is the memory I have. What strikes me is I have another, far more sinister memory.

I remember, I think, stepping off the school bus on the road outside the train station near to where I lived. I remember speaking to Kim, or some other school friend I was experimenting with, before setting off home for dinner. To my left, a figure approached me wearing a camouflage bomber jacket and lightweights, riding a racing cycle painted enamel green. He spoke to me in a soft voice, a charming and genteel man, and grabbed hold of my collar, before telling me he was going to fuck me. Thinking I was in some major trouble, I ran away from the unknown figure all the way home, to find my mother having a ball of a day and dismissing my complaint about the strange man as make-believe. Realising I would get none of her concern, I retired to my bedroom to skulk alone. Outside the figure rolled to a steady halt immediately in front of the house and looked up and in, right at me.

I had never felt fear before in my life, except when I knew I was going to get a hiding from my father for breaking something of my brother's. Strangely, I remember not knowing what emotion I was feeling. I was shocked by my mothers lack of care, shaken by the strange man's approach, and confused by the threat of someone wishing to harm me. I confess it here, and remember that I am not perfect myself. In later years as I reached my 30th birthday, I too could recognise I had also developed some perversions I found difficult to dismiss as harmless amusements. I saw the terror in each boy's eyes as I searched their soul, looking for some recognition of the pain I felt as a man. Though none could see or believe in the life behind my eyes, all could see my shame. It was only too well known in the community of adults where I resided. An outcast, a danger, a threat, a problem, a pervert: potentially a paedophile.

The boot may be on the other foot. But my parents couldn't care less if she had planned what happened soon after.

This game of cat and mouse went on for weeks at a time as he preyed on my vulnerabilities. Often afraid, eventually I confronted the stranger with all the wit and determination of Scrappy-Doo. Unfortunately for my innocence this was in vain, as his age overpowered me, and that evening he arrived on my doorstep with the express intention of taking me out some place I had never been before. Terrified, I followed him nonetheless, as I had nothing else to do, and besides he had gained my admiration in the weeks that had precluded my coming of age, as he was determined as a cat trying to break into the lair of its mate. Besides, my parents believed he was a young man of good character and probably thought it was for the best.

As soon as I had waved my mother goodbye, we set off.

We set out in the direction of the City, to see an old Co-Ed's of Simeon's, who would later turn out to be a pornographer and computer whizz. I followed him through the back lanes of the countryside for 8 – 10 miles, puffing and panting all the way, trying to keep up. Every so often he would call back for me to keep pushing ahead, sometimes dropping back to follow me from behind. So far into the journey, I was enjoying the company of this rather attractive and debonair gentleman. He was taking good care of me and all my fears and anxieties dissipated in the warm evening breeze as we rode headlong into the sunset dead ahead…

On our arrival at the intended destination I was left at the gate of a property just on the outskirts of the city, while Simeon called for his friend. Soon a bedraggled and rather green looking youngster came to the doorway. He was fat and blond, spoke in a West Country accent and was dressed like he was Worzel Gummidge.

A conversation ensued, and I was called from behind the picket hedge, out of sight and down the path to where the two of them held their beers close to their chests.

Steven, the boy I had not recognised as my earliest childhood friend, was suddenly shaken by my appearance and hid behind the alcove of the doorway with a cry of fright. Simeon called out to him to come back and face his new friend. Still unaware I had met my primary school friend, he crept out of the shadows and timidly made his greeting.

The first question he asked of me was;-

'Have you ever seen any teen porn?'

I had not. I was about 13 years of age after all and I was not interested in any girls at the time. I had already done what was required of me by losing my virginity and at this moment I was more interested in Simeon... Somehow, that much still figures.

Simeon smiled right at me, assuring me there was nothing to fear here. I asked for a beer of my own.

'Sure.'

I added my tuppence to the conversation as the two of them spoke at length about college, pornography and a new phenomenon I had not even heard of; LSD, or 'acid' as they called it.

Steven went inside and came back with a parcel made from a folded piece of glossy card. Offering it to me, he asked if I wanted to try his drug of choice. I opened the wrap, but failed to see anything inside. Confused, I handed it back to Simeon who placed some part of it in his mouth and told me to put my tongue out. Placing his finger on my tongue, he told me to swallow and thank him later.

I had no idea what to expect. I was just agreed to be complicit in whatever happened next.

The conversation continued between Simeon and Steven while I fussed over Steven's dog, Marley; a huge beast of a dog, a husky or some other far eastern animal that was fierce and yet intelligent. As I did, some force of nature came over me. My head was filled with loving thoughts of the girl I had experimented with and my heart warmed to the erotic thoughts I had held dear to my identity.

By now, from the doorstep, Simeon was encouraging me to get a computer and join them in their full time hobby. I dismissed his insistence, telling them both my father would never agree to it, when at that moment my father's voice emanated from out in the lane.

'Shane!' I could hear him call.

Stunned, I asked when were going to leave. Simeon gave Steven the nod and sat astride his bicycle. Smoke reached my eye from Simeon's cigarette – I didn't smoke yet and I wiped tears from my eyes with the sleeve of my jacket

'Now' he said, and we were gone, back into the dead of the summertime evening along the lanes to our destination on the Stanney estate: Kenilworth Court.

The scene was set for many more years of wandering the roads of Cheshire with these two young hippies.

And that is what went wrong. I don't doubt it any more and I am as ashamed as he still is. Thankfully, we stay out of each other's way now. I am strong enough to defy his will, but still not yet my own.

The story doesn't end there though. Simeon and I went on to become firm friends for many years after, right up until my breakdown in the winter of the year 2000, when we exchanged some hostile words about each other's bad habits. They were words that sorely needed to be spoken. After all, in the 6 years we had known each other I had never really grown to like or trust him as I should have. We had completely opposed ways of thinking and acting and could not agree on anything. Quite literally, we were at each other's throats. Besides, he had a growing family by then with a teenage daughter, and me being twenty years of age, I was a serious threat to his family's security. And he could see the progression my illness would take with one swift and canny answer to the question I had been harassing him with for years.

'Go and see Kim...' he asked of me one afternoon in summer after I had ingested a hallucinogenic mushroom. I was stumped by his proposal.

'What do you mean?' I begged of him several times to no avail. He would not let me into his little secret living next door that I had allegedly been searching for my whole life.

Unfortunately, I had no recollection of any neighbour of his that I might like to meet. And on his word, I left his home never to return to visit my now long missed friend of many years.

So, what did I do? The result of this one pivotal day in my adolescence began the destruction of my gender role within the confines of my relationships and the instruction of the authorities to clamp down on my more exuberant personality traits that not even I would admit to, not yet anyhow.

So where to now?

I first started to be treated by a psychotherapist in the winter of 2000. I had no idea why I was under such a terminal institution as the local health authority, but it suited my purposes. I was kept in a hostel in the inner city of Chester, and interviewed by my psychiatrist at regular intervals. Her primary concern was not my health but my safety. In the world I had become ensconced in, I had become a liability. My friends, love them or hate them, were more criminal than I gave them credit for and looked to me with jealous eyes for having been given the green card by the police after leaving psychiatric care.

I was a free man: or at least so it seemed.

My life, however, was still in jeopardy. In spite of my confused sexuality it was alleged I had children of my own. I dismissed the rumour as a lie, probably spun by a cheating ex-partner of a friend. If it was true, I really had been cheated from the moment I reached puberty.

My paranoia was tantamount to the rage I felt as a young man.

I had become Simeon.

0. The Beginning

I remember the stories my mother and aunt would tell me about our grandfather as a child. He was in the Luftwaffe during the Second World War, they would tell us. He was shot down in his Messerschmitt near the marsh adjacent to the ship canal, just a few miles from where we lived. Still, his aircraft remained half-buried under the carpet of grass, beneath the embankment where I came to stand one day in the early winter of 2002, looking for some solace from the world.

Underneath the lichen and green weeds the rusting hulk of aircraft lay undisturbed for over 60 years before I discovered it. The tail end of the plane was all that there was to see. The rest had sunk into the marsh or was under the flow of the water and had almost completely rotted away. At first I didn't realise what I had found. I assumed the rusting metal beneath my feet right at the corner between Weston Point and the Weaver navigation was nothing at all peculiar. I didn't even notice it. It was years later, when my mother mentioned that her father was buried at the local cemetery, that the thought occurred in my mind and I wondered whether I should return to the place I found that day and discover, for myself, what Victor's legacy to us all really was.

But that was many years later...

In the summer of 2001, I was living the high life in the city of Chester, in a hostel for the students at the University. I was suffering, to be true, with mild depression and a bout of loneliness after another failed relationship and was as horny as a lamb's hunger to find myself living out the situation I was in. I spent all my free time plotting my escape and shovelling shit up my nose to relieve the boredom of having no life's purpose.

Shane Leah

During this period my sole friends were my aunt Barb and her husband, Fergus. One an old witch of a bag lady, t'other an old fag. They met in the summer of '73 on Dukes Drive, an old rear entrance to Eaton Hall where the Duke of Westminster's family seat was situated. They had hung a painting of the scene they inhabited that day on the wall of the stairs. All earthen colours, oranges and browns that never faded, the blue of a late summer evening, the green of weeds. In amongst the trees, balloons were caught up in the branches while below a man in a daffodil yellow shirt danced with arms raised, right in front of a chequered towel laid out for a picnic.

The picture was very reminiscent of the personalities that crowded the house, not to mention the colour scheme of the house itself. It was dark humoured, dirty and with a morbid, blood red fascination with what had been lost.

She told me the painting was created by a friend of hers, who made off with her stash back in the 60's. The artist had painted herself into the crowd, leaning on a book, pencil in hand, making a sketch of the party. 'That was Jude…' she would tell me.

'An excellent artist.'

I agreed.

This was the sole image in the house.

Of course, times were hard in the Klosowski-Travis household. Money was tight, her only daughter was often sick and had many complex needs. Not to mention her drunken, drug addled, out of work husband who remained idle most of the time except to go out on drinking binges with his gay mates from town. Fortunately, by this time, I was one of them.

Fergie, as we called him, had been married for 36 years at the time of this story and had been a father for 17 of them. Being a father made him an exceptional character in my eyes. His wisdom saved my sanity many times before I reached 30. Fergie, you see, treated the women in his life with the contempt they meted out to him. I always liked to see myself as a sweet, honest, clear headed character. And I loved women, or so I would have liked to believe. My behaviour belied that of course, as I was never seen with any women other than my mother, and of course Fergie's long suffering wife, Barb.

And like Barb, some part of me was crying out loud for some 'thing', person, sign, symbol or answer that would inform me as to how I might continue to live in freedom from the demands being made of me by my defeated ego.

And so here I was, on 'His Lordship's Lane.' Once a 19th century furlong, I was standing on my grandfather's grave.

Across the canal itself, high up above the line of sight, I could just make out the landing strip of Liverpool John Lennon Airport. Much closer than that though, on the marshland separating the tidal waters of the River Mersey from the ship canal, I could make out a herd of cattle approaching me.

Surprised by the entrenched site of the cattle, I stood and fixed my gaze on the herd and imagined to myself that I might be peering through some camouflage netting hiding a territory beyond the sandbanks of the river. At that moment, I caught sight of a flash of white light above me. There was the sound of a metallic crease, like a creaky door opening, and the ground beneath my feet gave way.

My right foot was now in the canal. I leaped backwards, stumbling and tripping, and fell over on my arse. My shoelaces had become caught in the twisted, rotten metal that lay below the waterline. Shimmying forward on my spurs, I pulled at the lace, breaking it in the process, and pulled my foot out of the dirty brown water.

I cried out loud.

I realised that this piece of grassland appeared to rest on top of the canal itself, like a jetty. I thought I'd better remove myself from this jeopardy and tucked my shoelace away, then crawled backwards like a crab over the moss covered turf that gave way each time I placed a hand or foot down. When I reached the embankment I could see that the carpet of moss and weeds weaved and bobbed about like a rubber mattress above the waterline. Given the mood that brought me here, it was a lucky escape from an unfortunate death.

I scrambled up the embankment in the direction of the lock keeper's cottage, to find a figure much like my own father in appearance, leaving it. Situated on the higher ground of the marsh, I stumbled along in the direction of the cottage over a field littered with sheep droppings. As I neared the lock keeper I called out and waved my hands above my head trying to get his attention. He did hear me, I was sure of that, but ignored my calls and drove away in his Land Rover. By the time I reached the fence on the road, he was a trail of dirt and dust.
It took me till 9pm to walk the 18 miles home, zig-zagging all the way.

1. Roman Bridges

The river that ran through the brush at the back of the racecourse turned at a right angle at the golf course and then travelled steadily out to the estuary up the canalised strait away from town and towards the hills from whence it came. Like a stream of life, it carried with it all manner of insects and animals, not to mention all the silt that had accumulated on the banks of Parkgate. From the brush at the back of the racecourse to under the rail bridge where the path allowed a passage for dog walkers to let their pets foul the pavement, the river ran deep and quick. From the river bank, the dark brown shade of the water racing in torrents of swirling currents gouged a wide channel of trepidation for those who trampled through the weeds and reeds to get a closer look at what was written on the far bank under the rail bridge. I guess I was the only person to do that. And as the Dee flowed from the weir upstream to the turn in the river where the 19th century engineers had cut a channel to change its course out to the sea, the erosion on both side of the banks uncovered many an interesting artefact from Chester's ancient history. Among them was the site of a Roman graveyard which was uncovered within the sandbank below; the high tide of the river flow. Forever lost, few people ventured there and knew what it contained. They simply cycled alongside the river, ignoring what lay below them in the silt and industrial waste that adorned the sandbanks at the river's lowest point. I made this discovery years later after I had travelled the course of the river looking for a place to lose myself in a pathetic state of romantic melancholy, searching for something to satisfy my meanderings on how to spend my life in comfort, wholly happy within myself. I never suspected the innocuous twig I picked up that day from the side of the riverbank to be anything other than a curious shape

with which to make a new sculpture in the comfort of my
bedsitter on the far side of town.

The day was bright and, having nothing to do, I scoured
the small ads looking for the opportunity to earn some
extra cash mowing lawns or delivering papers, anything
really. Truly it was unnecessary as I was currently
unemployable due to suffering a breakdown the year
before, leaving me in hospital for 18 weeks while I was
assessed and given drug therapy to help with my
ailments. Within the confines of the asylum I had felt
comfortable doing nothing, but now I was out I was
itching for more to do than I could lay my hands on. I
wrote sometimes, played my guitar [badly], and went out
on walks around town – the park, the river and such.
Having no friends nearby and no partner with which to
spend my time I began looking for a new purpose in life,
something I could get my teeth into. Within the columns
of work advertised was an ad for an artist to paint a
mural on a garage door. It seemed an opportunity to
pursue my talents in an abstract fashion. I made a note
of the number and removed myself from the chair I had
sat in for weeks on end to get a beer from the fridge.
When I returned a figure loitered outside the window.
Behind the net curtains a woman was looking in before
moving away quickly. I went to the door, opened it and
peered out to the left. Moving away from me was a tall
blonde woman wearing a grey pen-line skirt reaching
down to the ankles, and a white blouse. I watched her
till she was out of sight and then returned to my can of
beer, wondering who was interested in peering in
through my window at 3pm in the afternoon and why?
Switching on the light I forgot about it

I reached for my artist's case and settled prostrate on
the floor with a blank canvas in front of me. Taking
some old photos of my nieces from the envelope I had

kept them in, I started to sketch out the outline of the youngest, head down with fringe covering her eyes. The lines I scrawled did not go down easily and I pressed hard on the paper to erase the mistakes. After an hour or two I had a good likeness of the photo down on paper and I took a break to grab a beer. When I returned to take out my oil paints and brushes I could hear the hollering sound of the boys from down the road pass the window and knock on the door.

I lifted myself to my feet and trod through the hall to answer the door. Neil, Tank, Dave and Damien stood outside in the fading light and asked if they could come in. 'Yeah' was my answer, and I led them into the living room. Showing them my recent effort lying on the floor they commented that it was looking good and sat down to build a joint. Talking animatedly amongst themselves, they debated the fate of a friend unknown to me; apparently he had moved his young girlfriend into the towers down the road and she had got pregnant. They doubted his good intentions, besides she was only fifteen and had left school to pursue her dubious first love affair against her parents' wishes and better understanding of the world. I doubted they cared much for her future, so long as she was not a burden to them. Fifteen seemed too young to leave home to me. By now the last of the joint had reached me and I filled my lungs with the sticky smelling roll before passing it on and trying hard to focus on the topic of conversation – I did not follow the words that came out of Neil's mouth or the replies from the rest of the group. I chose to ignore the conversation going on around me and rolled a joint of my own from the ounce of weed I bought each and every week for years from a dealer across town.

As I finished rolling a joint for myself the boys asked for some weed to go with to their next intended destination.

I obliged as I always did, and jumped to my feet and went to the kitchen to get a knife, returning to cut a large chunk of the block off for them, passing it to Neil. He didn't give any thanks, they never did, and then they rose to their feet and like a rugby scrum of 4 foot midgets raced for the door, falling out into the street making a loud commotion as they did. I closed the door and wondered why I bothered with them. I clearly needed the company of others since I had moved to this town, as I needed to make new friends after my early childhood friends had fallen by the wayside in my late teens, but I got no respect from anyone here. Except, that is, the barmaids in the Egerton, who were obliged to talk to anyone who cared for conversation.

The boys that had just left were a law unto themselves in this town. No-one could prevent them from terrorising the locality with their attitude and acts of intimidation as they hung out on the street peddling their dodgy weed. I certainly could not control them and pandered to their whims in an effort to stay out of trouble. Sometimes I tried to play the game like an eternal father, encouraging them to clean their act up and become good citizens, in an effort to calm my own troubled nerves when they became too rowdy. I tried, but it was no use; they had their own ideas about life and intended to pursue their gangster heaven. It was a knock to my ego to some extent, as they were nearly half my age and completely out of control. I certainly did not have nearly as much clout amongst the rocks by the waves in this town and I wondered if I had been as difficult as a child in my home town where I had started taking drugs early in my teens.

Propping up my nearly finished piece on the fireplace, I decided to take a walk to the garage where I assumed the piece was to be completed as a mural. I put on my coat, picked up my tobacco and phone and set out to where the old dairy once stood.

The old dairy was situated behind an old filling station to the west of the town, in front of the site of the old infirmary. As I approached the site I was cautious not to be seen ,as people lived right out front and would be suspicious of my character hanging out in a dead end street. In front of me, looking as derelict as the infirmary, was the tin roofed and enamel painted shed that had once been the site of my first ever job as a milk boy. A new sign hung above the shutter door for a local scrap yard dealer who I assumed had gone into business in vehicle repair. I pushed on past the buildings to the end of the street to see what lay behind.

To the back, the river ran in swirling currents of sand coloured swim. It had a peculiar smell, like you could smell the scent of the sea and the soil at once from the edge of the bank which was being eaten away by the rush of the river. Without proper defences against the tide, I guessed the building would be lost to the ever encroaching current. As I took in the senses I romanticised the backstreet scene as a place to work from. Outbuildings stood at the top of the lane and I was seduced by the thought of making a studio for myself here. As I did an old man stood on his doorstep behind me, watching me.

'Oi' he shouted to me. 'Who are you looking for?'

I replied that I was just checking out the area because I might have a small job here.

'Well, the dairy's closed,' he said, 'no use hanging around here.'

'Yeah, OK,' is all I said and turned to walk away.

He took a step inside and hid behind the door, watching me leave. I neared the end of the street and looked behind while the commuters passed in heavy traffic on the by – pass. The little old man was checking the shutter doors and locks. I looked to the left and to the right then crossed the road back to the derelict infirmary in St. Martins Fields through the gridlocked traffic, in front of the watching gaze of a face familiar to me but not one I recognised.

When I returned home I switched on the light and turned on the computer and searched the net for an hour or two. My horoscope could tell me nothing of the day's events other than the possibility of change in my life. I settled to make a single mark on the surface of the canvas I had earlier painted; a tear in my niece's eye. I then ran a bath, before preparing to retire to bed.

Behind the curtains, the woman I had seen twice that day was peering in through the gap, taking in the soul of the world I had created, unbeknown to my faltering conscious mind – though I did know, I chose to ignore it and left for the kitchen to make a late night coffee.

My father called at 2pm the next day. Already he had heard of my latest distraction to pursue a career in painting and was somewhat amused at my tenacity of spirit. He asked me about what I intended to paint and I showed him the painting of my youngest niece. He simply let out some stifled laughter and invited me to take a ride with him to see his friend across town. I gathered my things and stepped out of the door to join him in his car.

The journey did not take long, and I was surprised to park up near the site of the diary across town. Behind a branch of a legal firm and up the gravel track and to the right was the site of two Victorian terraces backing onto a sewage farm. We exited the car and approached the house to the left. On the drive in front stood an American motor-home, and a 4x4. My father went straight to the door and called while I peered into the window of the motor-home. A woman came to the door and let my father in; I sat outside on the bench and rolled a cigarette. As I smoked I took in the surroundings. To the front of me the river turned at 90 degrees towards the industrial units in Deeside, and a path ran alongside the bank of the river about 5 foot above the water. I stood and walked away from the front garden to the bank of the river.

From the bank I could see upstream to the site of the old diary and the back of the carpenter's workshop that jutted out in front of the lock gate that carried the canal into the river at high tide. I took a walk downstream to enjoy the rare opportunity of seeing some nature.

On the far bank, the golf course was quiet for a Sunday; I could see no-one on the 9th hole amongst the cherry trees and windfall pears. At the next turn in the river below the riverbank, a sandbank was raised above the flow of low tide, littered with industrial waste and fallen branches. I stopped and looked down at the assorted junk lying on the bank. Thinking ahead of my future career in the arts, I strode down the riverbank, clinging with my left hand as I went to the scrub and reeds that grew on it, to fetch a curious piece of wood I could see resting on the sandbank. Without getting my ankles wet I jumped over the stream between the riverbank and the sandbank and caught hold of the branch. Lifting it out of the sand, I washed it in the river and took a good look at it. It was a certain shape that was familiar, like a fused piece of anatomy, maybe part of a rib cage or something. I clenched it in my right hand and ascended the riverbank in the same manner I had made my way down, clutching at the reeds with my left hand and treading carefully up the incline.

Once I had reached the footpath I walked back to the house I had come from, pleased with my new discovery, with thoughts of setting down its form on canvas. I reached the end of the footpath and turned the corner to the front of the terrace and up to the door on the lean-to. I knocked and entered, following the sound of chatter through the vestibule and tentatively opened a door into a cosy living room with a red leather couch and fireplace. Sat at right angles to one another was my father and his friend, as of yet unknown to me, talking about cars.

Looking up from his place, my father asked where I had been. I told him I had simply taken a walk with my cigarette downstream.

'I had no idea the river ran out back.'

'What's that you've brought with you?' my father asked about the strange looking artefact hanging out of my pocket.

'Oh, I found it downstream. I don't know what it is, I was thinking about painting it.'

'Let's have a look.' I handed the twig to my father and he looked it over with increasing interest and worry.

'What's wrong? I asked,

'Oh, nothing - looks like an old Roman bone!'

'If it's come out of that river it probably is,' his friend said, 'there used to be an old Roman burial ground out there, just upstream.'

My father said 'Yep, they buried the plague victims there as well, St. Martin's Fields – you've been there haven't you?'

'Yeah,' I said – again laughter.

'Oh well, keep hold of it,' my father said, 'it's probably worth something to someone.' My father and his friend laughed between themselves again with a knowing glance and offered me a cup of tea, before venturing out to look over the motor-home.

We all clamoured around the motor home. My father's friend set about opening the door and switching on the ignition so he could show us its features. My father and I both climbed aboard and took a tour of the living quarters, kitchen, bed and shower. Lifting up a panel on the dashboard, he demonstrated the two way radio and CD player and switched on the air conditioning, all the while telling us of his trip to France with his wife. It was all dreams to me; I would never have even hoped to leave my home town in a hurry, let alone travel round Europe. Guess my dad felt the same too.

Having shown us both its inside, he suggested we take a trip to his place of work. Knowing he owned a garage and scrap yard, we hopped into the Ranger and made off in the direction of Queensferry. Soon my father was asking the old question about girls. This was a subject I hated, as I had been let down a lot in life and the conversation always hurt. I responded the usual tough way, choking back the feeling as best I could, 'Ahh, well guess I'll cross that bridge when I come to it,' were my words, and then I sat staring stony faced out of the window. His friend said something about my father having to do something, 'something,' I thought, 'whatever that something was.' I had no idea of the depth of feeling I shared that moment with the two other occupants. A silence ensued for the next 10 miles except for a comment on someone's driving.

We pulled up at a large farmhouse, not what I expected. I asked about the garage, only to be told we had taken a diversion to my grandparents. We hopped out onto a gravel drive and walked to the oak door. It opened immediately and we were greeted by the smiling elderly couple who welcomed us with open arms and ushered us inside. 'We have guests as well!' my Nan exclaimed. It was quite cosy to be treated as a 5 year old. We entered and I was told to sit in the breakfast bar and wait for a moment.

As I sat mulling over my thoughts I could hear a conversation going on out of earshot; joyous voices complimenting each other on their good fortune. I simply sat and waited to be called. Soon the voices travelled out of a door out of sight and I sat in the kitchen for what seemed like hours, alone. I turned on the small portable TV and watched an episode of some arts and crafts show shown on Welsh TV. I thought I had been forgotten about. I stepped down from my stool and peered around the corner of the kitchen door frame, looking for my father. No sign of him. Thinking nothing of it, I opened the barn door and stepped outside to make a cigarette.

I was standing in the spitting rain in the privy yard outside when my Nan appeared in the kitchen. 'No smoking here please,' she shouted. I immediately put out my cigarette on the floor without thinking of her reaction and stepped inside to apologise. As I did she rushed outside and picked the remains up off the floor and put it down the drain. Afraid of upsetting her again, I apologised once more before she began to ask questions.

'So sorry, we don't so that here, I forgot we had one more, would you like a cup of tea?'

'Yes,' I said.

'OK, one minute. Tell me, what is your name?'

I was confused by the question. I thought she had asked what the names of Robin's two children were.

'Unfair and untrue', I murmured on, thinking she had some suspicious thoughts about something.

'Sorry, what was that again?' she interrupted. Thinking she was troubling my conscience, I snapped back

'Neither of them are mine' I said. I felt sure of that.

'OK, tell me. Do you have a girlfriend?'

'No…, still looking.'

'Oh, never mind, I'm sure you will find a nice one soon.' She was just as patronising as my mother, never mind my father.

And with that she disappeared back into the house, out of sight. I made my own cup of tea in the end, because she didn't come back. Then my father appeared as if from nowhere, looking pretty pissed off. At first he just looked, then stared and pursed his lips. I must have done something wrong for him to be in this mood.

'What?' I asked.

He just shook his head and walked away. Next my Nan appeared. She said nothing, just looked and left. I could hear some murmurs in the breakfast room followed by my Dad's raised voice. By now I was getting agitated and stepped out into the foray to ask what the deal was. I was simply told to sit down. I did, and waited for my next instruction. My Dad was at the doorway again. This time he spoke.

'What's the problem with you, eh?' he asked. Shaken by the abruptness of the question I just mumbled some words.

'I don't know,' I said, 'what do you mean?'

He walked away again with a look of disgust in his face. Next my Nan was at the doorway.

'He's given up, love – I'm sorry.' I didn't understand immediately, but the heavy atmosphere told me all I did not hear. I sat looking between my knees at the floor, beset with negativity. I did know the story here.

'Dad..., I...' and with those words I broke down.

Soon my sister and her husband arrived with their two small children. I was surprised to see them here. I did not know this was some place they knew. I had finished sobbing and my father told me we were going for a drive. I asked where to. He just told me to get my coat and bring my branch with me. I got up immediately and followed him and his friend to the Ranger and settled in for the mystery journey.

The first few miles passed without a word uttered. I chose not to break the silence of the rumbling road and instead stared blankly out of the window experiencing waves of emotion, my folded arms clenched tight. I hid my one shed tear behind my arm with a gasp of breath. My father spoke first to his friend and then opened up the conversation to me.

'So, where are we going then?'

'Don't know,' I replied.

'Yeah. Hmm, so what is it your going to do with your life then?' and, before I could answer, 'Yeah, that's a question for you, yeah...' I didn't know why he was being so mean. There was no good reason for it. I sat silent for a moment and then, when I had suppressed the tide of anguish, I cleared my throat and answered in the most charismatically stable voice I could muster.

'I want to be a writer...' At least it raised a laugh, and with my two companions chuckling away to themselves I let out a smile too.

'What's this stuff about some painting your doing?' was his next question. I told them both about the opportunity I had seen in the paper to paint a mural on a garage door, and how I saw it as a meaningful vocation in which to indulge my passion for the arts.

A few words were exchanged between my father and his friend, and there were smiles all round.

'Well, that's where we're going then,' he said finally. I didn't quite catch hold of what he said and just sat back in my chair and relaxed, enjoying the ride.

Unexpectedly we took a diversion en route and climbed the hill to the Garden Village near the estuary and parked at the kerb. Here my father pointed out a house to his friend, asking him if the house was the same one he had dreamed of buying and restoring as a lad. His friend couldn't tell him. 'I don't think I knew you then, Shylock' he said. 'Have you thought about buying a house?' my father asked me. I answered a certain 'no'. 'You could probably afford one on your money,' his friend answered. 'I bloody well can't...' I doubted it myself. I had lived hand to mouth for years.

Suddenly we were off again, travelling back down the hill from whence we came, with no explanation of the events that just occurred. I just raised my eyebrows at the confusion I thought we all felt, and idled away with my own thoughts. As we entered the city again my father again started his rhetorical questions about my future.

'So, what are your plans for this place then?'

'What place?' He let out a sigh and continued to his friend that I was a bloody idiot.

'The garage...'

'I was going to paint a mural of baby Amy on the shutter door.' She was my sister's new baby.

'Why baby Amy?'

'It's the only good photo I had,' I said.

His friend nodded at my father 'Fair enough, yep.'

'I don't know...' said my father. A few brief words were exchanged as we passed the entrance to Peter's house.

'Do you know my friend?'

'Peter? Yeah.' I said.

'Good, because he owns the place.'

And with that we turned into the back street where the unit was situated.

I was surprised to be here with my father and his friend, as I had not expected my idle daydream of being able to paint a mural to be this easy to achieve. Obviously they had talked before of my passion for the arts and they both saw the circumstances surrounding our needs and wants to be mutually beneficial.

In the daylight, the old dairy that was now Peter's garage had become a blank canvas to me. A little apprehensively I exited the Ranger and stood in front of the shutter doors, admiring what had become my latest inspiration. I felt the excitement of creation running deep within me, and followed my father as he walked around the corrugated steel walls, looking for the door inside. My father told me to wait at the front for them to open the shutters as they entered by a side door in the wall.

I stood out front, taking in the scene of my creative venture. Just like last time the little old man from the terraced houses was peeping out at me from behind his net curtains. I turned to look back at the shutters, planning the use of spray paints to transcribe the painting I had done of baby Amy. I could hear the voice of my father and then the shutter door opened slowly, half way, to reveal Peter pulling on the lifting gear to raise the door. I entered the unit, finding all the equipment for the start of business ready to be used, including the pit in the ground for working underneath a vehicle.

'So, what do you think?' I was asked

'Well, I was thinking of using spray paint and touching it up with enamel poster paint to define the edges.'

'Don't use poster paint,' I was told, 'it'll run as soon as it rains.'

'Yeah, probably.'

'OK then. You're on...' Peter said, and then moved towards the back of the shop.

My father and his friend talked amongst themselves and I took a walk outside to the back of the shop to stand by the river. I sat on the bank, with my feet dangling over the edge of the water, staring into the dark brown swill. I put my hand into the pocket of my coat and pulled out the piece of branch I had found down river earlier. I admired its form; it was such an inspiring shape, with flakes of bark peeling from the smooth underside, like a carved curiosity from some artist's portfolio; maybe a master craftsman's initial ideas for a surrealist installation.

My father appeared behind and sat next to me. He asked what I was doing.

'Just looking at my twig,' I replied. He stared at the opposite bank.

'Do you know what this place used to be?' he asked.

'Yeah, a dairy.' He let out a stifled laugh.

'No, this is St. Martin's Fields, this place is.' I had heard him talk about this place earlier.

'Yeah, I know.'

'Let's have a look at your twig then.' I handed him my curio and waited to hear what he would say. He gazed long and hard at the smoothed shape I had fetched from the sandbank, turning it over and over, and then threw it with a passion into the river.

'Oi, I wanted to keep that!' I said as it plopped into the swell. Disappointed to lose my newest plaything, I watched it carried off downstream.

'I used to live near here as a kid, you know.' He started to roll a cigarette.

'No I didn't, when was that?'

'Bloody hell, when the dinosaurs roamed the earth.' I laughed. My father still treated me as a child.

'This used to be a smallholding. That barn,' he pointed to the left where an old outbuilding had been converted into a house, 'was old Nell Crookshank's farm. There used to be an old cottage next to it where he lived...'

'...Gone now like. That barn must be 150 years old.' He continued to stare at the opposite bank with a glazed look in his eye.

'Yeah, old Nelly Crookshank...'

'What do you know about him then?' I asked.

'Yeah…' Is all he would say, and sucked his teeth with a rasp.

I could hear the shutter doors close with a bang behind me and we both stood to leave as Peter exited the side door.

'All right, ready for the off?' Peter asked.

'Yep,' my father replied, and we made our way to the car. I sat inside while my father and his friend hitched up a trailer filled with scrap from the garage to the towbar and then joined me inside. As we started down the road to the junction, my father asked if his friend knew anything about Nell Crookshank.

'Yeah, I knew him.' He said.

'What did he do back then?'

'Oooohhh, don't ask.' They both chuckled a little before a disparaging silence ensued.

A few hundred metres passed and again I had no idea where I was going to, with the trailer towing behind. Soon I could tell by the atmosphere in the car that something was up, and so I asked what was bothering them.

'Nothing… ' my father said, 'Nell, he was trouble…' His friend just nodded in agreement, let out a gasp of air and gave his left eye a rub.

'What did you know about him?' my father asked his friend.

'His kids...,' answered his friend as he studied the road ahead.

'Yeah, do you reckon he did it?'

'Yep, definitely, they found him out in the end.'

'Found what?' I asked. I was curious by now of the depth of conversation they were having.

'Your aunt... when she went missing, years ago... Do you know why?' he asked Peter.

'Yeah...' He let out another sigh, and in a whisper said, 'He got her pregnant, what are you supposed to do?'

'Yeah, that's what I heard, when I got back.'

I clamoured for the gossip, asking what the story was, eager to learn what they had to teach me. My father stuttered and mumbled his words at first, as he always had found the past difficult to talk about and here was no different.

'Well in the 60's..., he started to talk.

'When was the 60's?' asked his friend. They both laughed.

'Were you there?' (My father).

'No, neither was I.' Again laughter, which surprised me, given the depth of the conversation.

'Yeah, the 60's, what about them?' I asked.

'Well, Nell you see..., he was a bit of an evil man and none of us knew it.'

'Why, what did he do?'

'He abused your aunt and probably your own mother. She was probably pregnant with his child at the time...'

I couldn't help but laugh. I had not heard anything like this before. Not from my father. I asked how he came to find out. He told me that when they came to build the dairy in the '70's, the contractors found two skeletons buried behind the barn to the left of the dairy. At first they thought they had once been plague victims, or maybe there was once a Roman burial ground there, with it being St. Martin's Fields. But no, the excavation led to an inquest and then a murder inquiry. But of course old Nell was long gone by then. But not before he had reached his retirement age. 'How he got away with it,' my father said, 'I don't know.' I asked why he murdered the two of them. 'So his son couldn't tell, I suppose, because he would have said something eventually.'

By now we had reached Bumpers Lane and the scrap yard. We pulled into the gate and I was told to wait in the car while Peter and my father unloaded the trailer. Amidst the crashing of metal plates and oil drums I rolled myself a cigarette and smoked it. A tap on the window from Peter told me to put it out. 'Don't smoke in the car!' he shouted at me. Outside in the yard an asylum seeker looking like an Afghan refugee was welding some angle iron together in some form of fabrication for the gates, I assumed, and two pit bull terriers were tied to a kennel barking with the chains that held them there at full stretch. Soon they were back in the 4X4 and back on the road, again to an unknown destination.

We left the town that bore all of us in silence. I didn't ask where we were going to, I just buckled in and sat back and relaxed. My father was the first to speak, but not to me.

'Who's that he's got working for him then?'

'The Afghan?'

'Yeah, the grease monkey in the rag top.' Both let out a cheer. I don't know what they had to celebrate.

Amidst the laughter I asked about Nell. Who was he and what was he? I didn't think I was being nosey, I guess I just wanted to be in on the conversation. He responded with a rebuttal. 'Oh, I don't know, what do you know about Nell?' he asked his friend. By now I could tell that he was holding something back I thought I needed to hear. I guess I should never have asked.

'How do you like Chester then?' my father asked. He wasn't giving anything away for free. He was normally this kind of man, full of difficult questions and whispers out of earshot; a very private individual.

'It's all right...'

I could hear my father's thoughts, comparing me to Kevin the teenager. I felt a little out of sorts from this discrimination, like I wasn't man enough to ride with the boys, even if they were both in their late fifties. Peter answered, saying he liked the place and had no problem with living there. I had my reservations myself; I wasn't at all happy there. I was lonely, away from close family and I certainly had no friends, though I had got to know the local fraternity of decrepit villains and drug users.

My dad probably knew it but couldn't care for his young son grown a man any more. My elder sister would never have shared such sensitive emotional stirrings in her soul. Neither would I.

My father continued his talk as we hurtled down the motorway towards Warrington, taking each turn in the road at top speed. He told me of his own experience of youth as he chatted with Peter about times long gone, carved into the furrow of his brow.

He had spent his own youth in the care of the local authority as his mother unfortunately became pregnant with him due to a drunken night out grieving for the loss of her fiancé during the war. She was incarcerated in an institution of some sort and he was eventually put into the care of his grandparents who were very understanding of their daughter's indiscretion. (As both were born in the 19th century, he told me, they had suffered far worse fates than that of being a single mother.) They took good care of his welfare and after a period of time his mother was married to a local man who took her on and they moved away, leaving my father behind until he was able to take care of himself, whereupon he moved away too to join them in their love nest in the north west. My father seemed upset to bequest to me such a hard luck story, but soon he was in good spirits again and joking about the past.

What he told me got me thinking about my own failure to gain the support I needed to make my life acceptable to those I had taken hold of in life. I sat comforting myself with delusions of what might yet be, but not known as of now. By that I mean what I wanted and how I had hoped to make my gains concrete. I had hoped for a loving partner and a family once, and thus by default had neglected to indulge my sexual frustration in any way other than pornography and occasional one night stands with cheap whores I could afford to hire from other out-patients on the ward I had stayed on as a broken hearted teenage dufus. It seemed remarkable that all my attempts to bring my urgings to procreate into reality had fallen by the wayside as I continued unabated to satisfy myself with teen porn and fantasies of schoolchildren. In my humble opinion I was doing nothing morally repugnant, though I was struggling to make my needs known outside of my tiny bubble.

By now we were in the suburbs of Warrington, and as we passed along the avenues towards our unknown and yet intended destination I recognised some of the landmarks from previous years. Soon we were pulling up outside an abandoned chapel on a main road near the river that flowed through the town. Here we jumped out of the 4X4, and while Peter went to attend to some business, me and my father wandered around the abandoned graveyard looking for familiar names on gravestones.

One epitaph read, 'Here lies Samuel Downs, Captain of the Salacious Whim, much admired and respected by all.' My father was amused by the caption. I failed to recognise its meaning and we moved in different directions, looking for a family name we did know.

Peter was still inside the church, which I had assumed to be a builders' yard, while we looked over the ageing tombstones laid over the earth as paving stones. Through the dirt and eroded sandstone I could just make out the name of Leah on a tombstone laid flat on the floor. I called my father.

'Here, Dad. We've got family here.'

He came over, asking what I had found. I showed him the inscription and read it back to him.

'Here lies therein the body of dearly deceased husband and father, Manny Leah, died Wednesday 23rd October 1872 off Liverpool Bay in stormy waters. Parent of two children, Annabel and Danny Leah, lost Sunday 17th August 1880 en route to Canada. Forever lost but not forgotten. Also, Elizabeth Cook, widow of Manny Leah, died 1st November 1888 after prolonged illness.'

'Could have been me that...' my father said. I had no idea what he meant. Instead, I asked him why there were so many merchant navy graves here, and we discussed the port of Liverpool just up the carriageway. From what he told me it would appear Warrington would once have been a thriving coach town en route to the seaport. Surprised, we continued our tour of the site. While I rolled a cigarette my father took in some more historical graves. Eventually he called to me to come over. We stood in front of an impressive stone tombstone inscribed;

'Entombed within, lies the remains of the body of Nell Crookshank, Blacksmith, chaplain of St. Martin's Infirmary, Chester, and previously, Sheriff of Wigan. Died the night of 3rd February 1973 at his home in Chester...

...Buried here with his brother Les Crookshank from Wigan. Died 19th April 1951 after succumbing to death by hanging at Walton gaol.'

I wondered what he made of the epitaph. Given all he had told me earlier I imagined a less grandiose grave would be appropriate. He queried the account of his brother being hanged at Walton and that's all. I asked him if he knew old Nell was buried here, and he replied a simple 'yes.' Meanwhile, as we stood gazing at the stone tablet, Peter returned from inside the building and called for us to make our way back to the car. Once inside we started off back to whence we had come.

As we left the town, the feeling of melancholic depression was all around, an atmosphere of being alone with just our thoughts. I sank into my seat and wondered what all this meant. Something was afoot involving my father and his friend and old Nelly Crookshank, though I could not work out what or why. Upon considering why I felt this alone, I went deep into the being of my soul to tease out my desires and whims and fears. I sat silent for the whole of the journey in quiet contemplation while Peter and my father were still talking about the history of their home town, laughing about falling out of trees and nearly drowning in ponds and so on. I reminisced about my own recent childhood doing the same idiosyncratic things. I thought to tell them of my own knocks and bumps, but didn't think it would raise a laugh, and so gave up the idea of trying to entertain their humour and instead listened hard to the chatter, failing to understand any of the sentences exchanged.

The miles passed on a rumbling road without a thought for the two people in front. I was considering telling my father about my feelings as they were right now, about feeling fed up with my miserable attempts to get myself noticed by girls, the suspected pregnancy I had recently been told to keep quiet about, and the issue of my fondness of the young girl who lived next door to me; I had lost myself in the emotion that came over me and completely forgot about the message of Nell. As the car exited the motorway back into Chester, my father turned to me with a tear in his eye and said; 'Well, what have you learned today?' I could not reply as I would have liked to and choked back the tears inside to hide my fears for the future. I knew here something was not being told – but I did have answers.

'I got a girl pregnant,' I whimpered rubbing a tear from my eye while they stared at the road ahead. Both my travel companions laughed out loud.

'You have, have you?' I could see him cry with laughter. His friend, recognising I cheered up in response to the commotion going on, cried;

'Get your knickers on you slag and pack your bags, I've had enough!'

'No,' my father said, 'I don't think.' The messages from the two of them seemed to conflict and again I felt confused. The thought pattern being; 'I don't want a child, I don't have one, but I do, and that's not right, but it's OK anyhow.'

'Anything else on your mind today?' was the next question. I didn't dare say what I was really thinking and spoke in euphemisms about the girl next door, the one who passed by outside my window every day at three o'clock.

'The girls just aren't interested in me, and when they are I just can't reach them. It's like I am banging my head off a brick wall.'

'How old is she?' my father put to me.

'Don't ask.'

At first there was a startled pause, maybe deciphering the content of the sentence I had just put to them, then the response came too quickly;

'Hillary... Yes.'

I didn't hear it the way I would have liked. I wasn't even sure I heard it. It simply wasn't the answer I had expected. Really, given the depth of the issue I would have maybe preferred a different answer, like no. I took a few minutes to consider the meaning of the answer, before accepting the plea for clemency. I recognised the reply and took its meaning as the truth. Though it did settle in my heart suddenly, by the end of the road it just tickled like mad.

Back at the shack, where the old dairy once stood, Peter turned the car around and unshackled the trailer, leaving it to the left of the unit. Climbing back into the car he said the trailer should be safe for one night and we left to return to the house he lived in behind the water treatment plant. As we turned into the drive that led up to the terrace my father asked me about the tombstone with our family name on it.

'What did it say again?'

'Something about a guy called Manny who was drowned at sea, in Liverpool Bay.'

'Yeah,' he said and he asked his mate, 'Do you remember being in Sea Scouts, and the trip to Ireland?'

'Yeah' he said. He began to tell his story;

'When we were kids,' he said, 'we didn't have the kind of things you lot have today.'
I agreed; I could see he was from a bygone era of innocence and poverty. At least that's what I told him.

'No,' he retorted, 'the Sixties, they were mad.'

'We were in the Sea Scouts...' his friend told me.

'Yeah!' My father let out a cry of joy. 'We used to sail boats on the Dee there.'

'D'you remember scrawling your name on the wall of the railway bridge?' Peter asked.

'Yes, I got grounded for that.'

We were still sat in the 4X4 at this point, looking out onto the front lawn of the terraces as the rain began to fall lightly on the wind shield in a pitter-patter fashion. My father was still talking about his youth in the Sea Cadets, and a trip to Ireland that went horribly wrong when the ship ran across a sandbank and got stuck in Liverpool Bay.

'What happened was we were coming home from a sabbatical with our Lieutenant and we got blown off course and hit a sandbank near Lancashire...' he was telling me. 'The ferry was spinning round in a vortex caused by the waves hitting the starboard side.'

'I thought we were going to die' Peter added.

'Yeah, when it hit that sandbank the whole boat shook like it was coming apart.'

'I thought we were going down.'

I fawned an expression of amazement at the story I was being told. It was some adventure they had had, for sure. But my father hadn't finished yet, and the story continued.

'The Air Rescue had to be called to lift some of the people off the ferry. We thought the Aliens had landed!' He chortled to himself in a fit of laughter.

I was amused by his synchronicity in my own mind; what with the tombstone of a family member who died at sea, my father being in the Sea Cadets and running aground off Lancashire and the tale of old Nell, the murderous chaplain who buried his children next to the banks of the river, Aliens went down easily.

And so we left the car outside the drive and ventured inside for a hot cup of tea. Peter's wife greeted us at the door and put the kettle on and we sat in the living room waiting for the tea to be served. My father continued to talk of his youth, with Peter solemnly responding to his memories of his first job at the diary, where we had been earlier, and now his latest business venture; his school friends from forty years ago whom he had lost touch with; and his first love; Alison Crookshank, my mum.

I missed the tail end of the conversation and failed to hear the name of Crookshank mentioned, until Peter asked if I was getting this. I mumbled some words of apology and sat up straight to hear the story being told.

'Nell? Yeah, he has told me.' Peter gave me a cold look.

'No that's not what we were talking about.' My father continued the discourse.

'What do you know about him?' he asked.

'Only what you have told me.' I replied. 'He murdered his two kids.'

'And that's not all!' cried Peter out loud. Even my father smiled with dry wit.

Suddenly Peter's wife entered the room to serve the tea and exited again. As soon as she was gone the conversation continued.

'It said on the epitaph that he was Sheriff of Wigan.'

'Once…, did you know that?' My father asked Peter. Peter nodded.

'Yes, I wonder why he resigned?' There were a few moments of silence before the conversation continued.

'Do you think he did it?' (My father).

'Could have been.' (Peter). Raised eyebrows all round.

I was beginning to get a picture of the story being told. I could have been mistaken, but I suspected Nell's older brother may have been a suspect for murder back in the late fifties. Maybe that's why he was hanged at Walton. My Hetty Wainthropp moment was interrupted by the phone ringing, and the voice of Peter's wife calling him to the kitchen. Peter left to speak to his wife and my father and I sat on the couch saying nothing to each other until Peter returned.

'Job's on' he said as he returned through the door.

'Have to get moving then.' My father waited a few moments, then got to his feet and followed Peter out of the door. I followed suit and they led me out the side door to the garden and the Winnebago. While I waited for instructions on where we were going next, Peter opened the door to the truck and let my father up the steps inside. While he showed my father how to start the engine and select the gears I peered in through the door, wondering what they were planning. Then with a roar of V12 engines, Peter told me to climb on board and buckle in for a journey. Startled by the events unfolding, I hopped on board and sat in the crew seat. Peter descended the stairs and closed the cabin door, and with a wave of the hand we reversed backwards into the lane nervously, taking care not to catch the gate post. Once around the corner, my father selected forward gear and we ambled on slowly with the power of V12 gas, down the lane to the right and onwards.

I started a conversation on my plans for the future.

'Tell you what Dad, I'm gonna' make a go of this life from now on...'

He ignored my comment and continued to focus on the road ahead.

'I reckon once I have painted the mural, I should go into collecting records and start a record company...' Again I got no reply. I continued my verbal diarrhoea.

'I could get a job at Virgin Megastore and learn the trade...' Here he stopped me.

'You know what, I don't think you will.' Confused by the rebuttal, I was about to defend my thoughts but he carried on.

'Have you given up smoking that shit yet?' – No, I hadn't. I chose to excuse myself.

'I am going to, it's just that sometimes I need it.'

'Yeah, whatever.' He let out a sigh of absolute frustration. 'I don't think you ever will.'

He seemed resigned to my long term drug habit. I had planned to change, just not today. I felt hurt by his abrupt challenge to my dream. I thought we were pals today and he would support my vision of how things could be. Not satisfied with condescending my efforts to impress, he continued.

'What did we talk about before?'

'Nell…'

'Yep, that's right.'

Just then a Bentley came charging down the opposite lane of the carriageway, taking up half of the white line marking the road. My father swerved to avoid a collision and we hit the kerbstone to the left, where my father was in his driving position. He pursed his lips in a rasp and made a comment about the driver 'taking us out' before pulling into a lay-by a few hundred metres down the road to check for damage.

We both exited the truck and travelled round to the left nearside to check the tyres and panelling. Neither of us could see any damage and so climbed back aboard to continue on our journey. Problem was, the bloody thing wouldn't start. My father turned the key and pumped the accelerator and still it wouldn't start. Confused as to what to do, he swore under his breath that 'we're fucked now' and pulled his mobile out of his pocket to make a call back to Peter.

Having told Peter we nearly had a collision, we were on the road again. I sat in silence, chain smoking roaches I had collected in my pouch that afternoon and admiring the view from the passenger seat. Suddenly my father spoke in an earnest tone.

'We were all really worried about you...' His voice quivered, only slightly, but I didn't recognise the real and genuine concern that was being offered from one generation to the next. I thought for a moment, though it escaped me; he sounded as solemn as I had ever known the straightest old man in the world to be. He even appeared to give the festering guilt I was so ashamed of a pat on the back for effort.

'Were yer?' I asked, not believing my ears.

He cleared his throat.

'Yes, really, we were,' he eventually said, in a clear voice.

Finally, we reached town again and I was glad to be invited this evening to a hospitable function at my uncle's house in the inner city. We approached Chester from the Broughton side and travelled through the Stadium Retail Complex into town.

The narrow lanes of traffic were difficult to navigate in the twilight. Each time we had to pass a vehicle we had to stop, select neutral and then pass the parked cars taking care not to hit anything on the right hand side. We passed the racecourse and travelled up the steep incline into town, took a left at the lights, then right at the roundabout, down the by-pass, a left at some traffic lights, and I was home again. I waved my father goodbye as he drove the Chevy truck over the railway bridge and away from the city down Hoole Road. I sensed something was wrong about the atmosphere between me and my father. We had not seen eye to eye today. We could not get along with each other at all on any terms. The thought that something may be wrong with my family dynamics tried to enter my conscious mind, but I instantly dismissed it as paranoid and continued my journey home to rest.

Caught with the indecision of getting some rest or going out for a drink, I decided not to go home and walk to the party at my uncle's instead. The streets of Chester were littered with the sprawl of festive teenagers, all binging on cider and vodka red bulls in bars all night, I presumed. The road I walked took me straight up through the Northgate Cross and back down the other side and along Garden Lane to where my friends were waiting.

I arrived at the door to my uncles' house at 12 midnight exactly, and knocked as I always did. There was a brief commotion behind the weather beaten door that had years of soot and grime all over its peeling and stained exterior. The family dog stayed strangely silent. Then, with a flash of light above my head, the door opened to reveal my uncle Fergus, looking tired and bedraggled, clutching a tin of Tennents.

'Come in, come in!' he called to me, and stepped back from the doorstep to let me in.

The whole family was still awake, and I was glad to see them. My aunt, uncle and cousin all gathered round me in the front room and asked me about my day. They seemed to have expected some impossible thing to have happened to me that day.

'Shane!' Fergus said, as I settled myself down.

'Any news on this new lady of yours then?' he asked.

'No,' I said. I didn't know what he meant.

'It's just that your dad said he had set you up with some gorgeous brunette babe!'

'No, haven't met anyone like that today.' I was tired of these wind ups by now and just brushed his insistence away with my hand to my face.

'So, you haven't gone and got married, then?'

'Nope.'

'Ahhh, well. It must have been someone else then!'

'Yeah, must have...'

And without even realising how stupid I had been, I went out of the front room to the kitchen, to fetch a glass of cider and chase Liz around the kitchen table.

2. 14 Years to Life

After waking from another debauched night of chain smoking weed and snorting fat lines of high grade cocaine, I lay on the couch at Robin's listening to the kids falling down the stairs at 7am to get prepared for school. Here, at the Territorial Army barracks, we could get up to whatever we wanted. The first house on the estate, it was well known by all who lived there what went on behind its curtains. I guess no one really gave a damn, after all, even in this quarter of town people needed an escape from the grind of life. As for myself, here at 23, I had tired of the constant battle of wills between Robin and her fella; my man, Ming; and myself. You see, ever since they had arrived in Chester, I had been under constant pressure from the two of them to feign my character and act as a father to their two children. Needless to say, I was reluctant to accept the rumour they insisted in stirring up with the neighbours, but as I practically lived there on the weekdays, I would simply ignore the words that were exchanged daily between the three of us in our ménage a trois, a modern family of three adults and two children under ten.

I was considering my feelings about this point of conflict when I heard the door slam closed, rattling the windows, and I could hear the voices of the kids trail off down the path with their mother. I didn't know why the two of them were passing the buck when it came to the kids. I guessed some other conflict was making itself heard in their lives that had not reached me yet. So it came as something of a surprise to me to find myself playing out this role under some exceptionally tenacious circumstances. I had no choice but to go through the motions of being a primary care-giver on a daily basis; though the disciplinarian in the family remained their paternal father, Ming, 'The Merciless.'

However, behind the cool exterior I demonstrated in my actions on a daily basis, I was a seething bowl of raging anger, fear and anxiety that only ever showed itself when I was sure I was alone. Anxious about the feelings of my friends, and more concerned about the thoughts of those I encountered daily in my occupation as a dope fiend, I would often scream out loud just to hear myself think. And when I was alone at home, at the hostel I had been lodging at since being discharged from hospital back when I was twenty, I would write my thoughts down as poems about my state of mind and dreams of the future I would have wished to create for myself.

I swung my legs off the couch to the floor and looked to my right, over the arm of the couch, to see the family cat race into the room from the hallway. A moment later, Ming entered the room with the bearing of a challenge. I looked up at his face, recognising the look he had of a hungry bear with a sore arse. He let out a noise to acknowledge my presence and went to the kitchen to find his bag. He returned to the room a moment later after some rustling of plastic and switched the television on. He got me up out off his throne by thumbing my arse out of his seat and throwing himself down in his usual laid back position, while I took up the Rizlas on the adjacent couch and put the first papers of the day together.

Ming flicked through the Sky channels and settled in to watch American Chopper. I checked the time on my mobile; it was 11.13am, later than I had thought. Ming looked over and asked what time Robin left to go to work.

'I don't know' I said, 'Earlier…'

'Bet she was late…'

Again? I thought. It would not be long before she was given her P45 and then they really were fucked. The rent on the terrace had not been paid in full in months and I was just waiting for their luck to run out. Ming, of course, saw the security of his tenancy as none of his concern. He after all could doss anywhere. He was as nonchalant about the security of the family, as I was mad about it. But underneath the calm exterior of our early morning psychedelic breakfast, both he and me were two extremely angry individuals, brooding over the fate that we had found ourselves obliged to live out in public.

Soon I was to find a lucky break through a spot of bother and a psychotic experience. Ming and his family however, were less lucky. They were to be locked up in an institution for homeless families with drug addictions.

But to see how this story begins, we must look back several years, to when I lived at my mother's and Ming and his family squatted in Robin's sister's bungalow in 'Tintown', to the west of my home town.

The story goes, back when I was a kid in the 90's, we were of a generation of young adults that gained some respect from our parents and elders for our opinions. Most of the adults in our lives respected our intelligence, being at school and all, and would encourage that flouting of 'alleged rules' to steel us for our future lifestyles. Maybe they were just obtusely permissive, or maybe even dumb. But what we learned about ourselves, in our liberal and intoxicated society, is that no one held a gospel on the truth. You must find your own for yourself. And that is what we set out to discover when my group of friends and the whole of our generation set about trying, using or abusing drugs.

This truth (and no one can deny it now), was reflected in the broadcast of channel 4's 'Pot Night' back in the late August of 1995. The programme, broadcast late at night on a weekday, was a revolutionary moment in Britain's legal and psychological history. The argument put together by the production team was that Cannabis Sativa and Indica, was an important social drug in many areas of Britain's society. They put it to the audience of about 10,000 that it had many medicinal and psychological properties that were beneficial to the user and it should be legalised. Pretty hot stuff!

And as this radical debate went on the screen of my best friend's television, I was passed a spliff. Not my first, and without thinking I ingested the whole thing to the roach and decided this was a defining moment in my youth. I can't say I never looked back; by the time I was in my twenties, I was suffering from a mental illness, brought about by years of chain smoking weed, having a dabble with coke and the people I was involved with as a result. But something I did realise, here in my older friend's flat, (who was later to become one of my school teachers), is that a cultural revolution had just awakened me to the life I should be living. A non stop 24 hour, mashed up, loony raving party. I thought to myself, you can keep the unbridled, passionate love and affection my then girlfriend offered and the commitment we were all expected to make some time soon. And instead, with my friend as my confidant and closest buddy come hell or high water, we set about getting the whole town stoned.

Needless to say, I soon lost my then girlfriend. Much to my disappointment, but I should have expected her not to follow suit, and do as I did. She was much more grounded and careful than me, not to mention scared. But I was full of spunk about my new identity as a stoner, and soon lost interest in her, (for a time), only to become increasingly more alarmed by the threat of my friend Simeon's developing sexuality.

So the weeks that followed were a breeze of late night smoke outs and wandering around town in our beige 1984 Ford Escort, looking for people who might be able to score us some weed. We never failed. I guess channel 4's Pot Night really was a reflection on a world I inhabited, but I never knew about. I was soon introduced to many more future friends and enemies that have made my life what it is today. All of them were to some extent involved or peripheral to the drug trade; including my old friend Ming, and his then teenage partner, Robin.

My mother, bless her, because she always has and probably always will look out for me, realised there had been a change in my personality in the past few weeks and months, and saw it as a good thing that I had found some real friends since I had lost my girlfriend, and was quite complicit in my assured future as a drug user. She could see I was being well looked after by my friend Simeon, and would do anything to allow us to continue to have a good time, even extend us money to buy more weed! Jesus, how much I loved my mum!

The whole message of this story, however, begins at the end of the summer term in school, aged 15, almost a year before my GCSE examinations.

Part of the curriculum for aspiring workaholic junkies in the school I went to, Bishops' High in Boughton, Chester – (I mention it just to disrespect it, then fall on my sword later in the story), was to commit to some work experience, in any area we might have been interested in. I chose to have two areas of endeavour. The first is not worth mentioning, except for the fact that my form tutor had got the sack and was working with me. It was a week long job working on a computer for a surveyors; really, very boring and monotonous work.

The second little job I had hoodwinked my way into was acting as a student of law, shadowing a Barrister on his work in the courts. I expected to be amazed by the complexities of legal procedure and the power this QC, and soon to be very famous political figure, had over the world. I was very excited about this appointment but unsure of what to expect, as I had never been to court in my life.

So when the day came, I woke early, shaved, bathed and set off to the chambers in Chester, where I was to find the lawyer that was to really unsettle all I had come to expect from the bright future I was sure I was part of.

I arrived at Stanley Place, by the racecourse at 9am prompt, Monday morning. Late of course, because of traffic, but I reached my fated destination with a great many interruptions. Upon speaking to the legal secretary I was led upstairs to one of the chambers, only to be turned away by a pompous looking man in glasses. Instead I was sent to Chester Crown Court, up the road past the old Cheshire Police Headquarters, to watch the procedure of a crown court trial. I had no idea what in hell was waiting for me there. But I went anyway. I still wish I had stayed at home.

I entered the court foyer from the public entrance, to the front of the building. Not knowing who to speak to or where to go, I first took a whizz in the restrooms before asking the staff at the diner who I should speak to about my entry to courtroom 3. One helpful member of staff directed me to speak to the Court Usher, a cloaked figure standing laughing and in deep conversation with a lawyer, in the middle of the foyer floor. I approached her tentatively to give the impression that I was new here and held some respect for those who inhabited its halls. As I did, the cloaked figure turned her nose up at me and moved away towards the courtrooms, down the main corridor towards the public gallery. I followed, trying to get her attention, but to no avail. She entered Courtroom 3 from the press gallery door, closing me out with an air of defiance.

Having found the right courtroom, I stood outside the press gallery door waiting for some figure or person to allow me in. An elderly man soon arrived and asked what I was doing. I explained I was here to shadow a Barrister on his work and learn about the courts.

'Defence or prosecution?' he asked.
'I don't know,' I said. 'Defence, I think.'

He told me I was in the right place and I should wait for someone official to let me in. He then explained he was just the janitor and that he couldn't allow me to wait here, before entering the courtroom and leaving me feeling negative about loitering outside the door.

I was about to leave at this point, when the Usher returned from the courtroom and asked what I was doing there, and I had to explain myself again.

'Well, I don't think we were expecting anyone except the witnesses' she told me.

I protested I was here legitimately and she left me waiting while she went to find out if anyone was expecting me.

Soon, a man in a suit and a well dressed and fragrant woman entered the court from the door I was waiting in front of. I attempted to gain their attention, but they pushed right past me, ignoring my attempts to engage them in conversation. Feeling defeated and confused by the hustle and bustle, I must have waited a nervous 10 – 15 minutes before thinking to myself that I must have got myself muddled, and walked around to the right of the courtroom looking for some other entrance. A few steps down the corridor I found a queue of people waiting to enter the Public Gallery of Courtroom 3. I asked one of the assembled crowd, a fat lady with blonde hair, if I was in the right place.

'Are you here to see it, too?' she asked.

I explained I was here to shadow a Barrister on his work in the courts.

'So you're a solicitor?'

'I'm thinking about becoming one...' I explained.

'Oh, good. You know what, this guy is going down today.'

'What for?' I asked.

'Murder...' she said, to a chorus of laughter.

I curled my tongue up against my back teeth and turned away for a moment, to hear an authoritative voice announce that Courtroom 3 was open for business.

The crowd of family members, neighbours and those with an interest in the murder case that was to be presented to the court that day, all steadily shuffled into the public gallery with an air of schoolchildren going to see a play, and I followed them with mild panic in my heart. Each of them found a seat on the benches, and I chose to sit right at the back of the gallery, so as not to arouse any attention.

The court usher stood in the middle of the courtroom and spoke to the secretary who was going to be taking notes 'verbatim', while the Barristers and assorted court staff organised their notes and files. Then with a flurry of excitement from the public gallery the Usher commanded the court to rise for the Right Honourable Mr Justice Terry, to take the stand. Unfamiliar with court procedure, I remained seated, idly watching the Judge enter the courtroom from his chambers to the rear of the bench. He looked just like the janitor who had refused to let me in, but he was wearing a grey shoulder length wig and silken robes. I remained sat down, until that is the court usher looked right at me and coughed, and then gesticulated for me to get up out of my seat, which I did immediately.

The Judge, adorned in a black robe and a grey powdered wig, bowed before the court witnesses and took to his seat in front of the Barrister's bench. The assembled court, Barristers, Jury and the witnesses let out a sigh of relief and mumbled to each other as they returned to their seats. I spoke to the person sat next to me to ask what the person on trial here today had done. I knew his name, Mark Dirom, but not the circumstances of the murder he had allegedly committed. Just as I had finished speaking the Judge spoke directly to me;

'Please, no talking on the public bench.'

Embarrassed by my blunder I blushed bright red and the guy I had just asked the question of shook his head at me.

'He hasn't' he whispered.

Confused by his reply, I looked around the court to find everyone's eyes on me for a moment before turning away.

Next the Judge whispered something to the court usher, and she replied in turn. One of the Barristers joined in the whispers to the front of the Judges' bench; then the Judge let out a cough and said:

'If there is a person looking to join the defence on their bench, please could you let yourself known to the court.'

I wondered if he meant me?

The Judge took up his glasses and placed them on the tip of his nose, before looking over the rim of them straight at me. I tried to avoid his stare and looked towards the floor. The whole of the public bench was now looking at me and I felt no choice but to raise my hand and explain my reasons for being there.

'No reason to explain...' he said, '...please exit the public gallery and go around to the right of the court and the ushers will let you in.'

I collected my bag and confidence together and exited the gallery to wait outside the Staff entrance to the court.

The usher let me into the Courtroom and sat me to the right of the stairs, on the press and witnesses' bench, rising up above the Courtroom floor, where I could look down on the Court and the legal experts gathered to testify their case. I placed my beige Hessian bag to the left of me, adorned with assorted schoolboy scribbles and graffiti, and cast my gaze over the people gathered in the court that day. I could see them all looking back at me, with mixed expressions of worry, amusement, malice and downright apathy.

I had already begun to wonder why I had been called to this courtroom, for this case, on this day. I remember the Barrister for the defence, and the Judge, looking me over with an air of pomposity, before bringing the court to order and calling for the prosecution to present their case.

The prosecution for the Crown was a tall, elderly man in his 70's, but in very good health. His black robes were made of a silken material and he wore a grey powered wig that dusted his shoulders with a fine chalk. He glanced over in my direction, held his clenched fist to his mouth and coughed, before opening his mouth wide and stating in very short and concise sentences the prosecutions' case.

In the prosecution's opening statement, the elderly Barrister told the court that the case was simple. The accused, the prosecution alleged, had left his home in Warrington in the autumn of 1994 to seek revenge on two men, Mr Murray and Mr Maguire. The prosecution's case was that the two men had received payment of £750 to attack a neighbour of Mr. Dirom's, from when he lived in Hampshire in the early 1990's. When the accused discovered the attack had not taken place, he asked for his money back, and the two men refused. Seeking revenge, Mr. Dirom had travelled from Carlisle, from Warrington, on the evening of November the 24th with a sawn off shotgun and brutally murdered the two men in cold blood, in front of their own home.

Captivated by the case put before the court, I watched, taking in the acute emotions of the public gallery. All of them were either baying for blood, or fools for justice. Several of them had just turned out for the sheer fun of seeing someone they had heard of get sentenced to life imprisonment. I recognised the professionalism of the legal staff and the innocence of the Jury; a collection of middle aged men on Jury service, an elderly man that seemed to fall asleep almost immediately and at least three women.

As I was listening to the defence put its case to the court, the accused, Mr. Mark Dirom, was led from the cells beneath the courthouse to the Dock, to be indicted.

He didn't seem like a murderer to me. In his new suit and polished brogues he gave an air of respectability and professionalism. He looked over the court from under a high brow of silent resilience. I admit I admired his good looks and calm demeanour. I was sure the defence might actually have a case that we might actually win.

And so, as the defence made its case that was to be presented to the court that week, the Barrister made it clear that the evidence they were to present rested on the account of a witness, who was alleged to have provided an alibi. The Barrister for the defence gave me a nod of his head and asked if I understood the court procedure. I agreed I did, certainly, and the court continued with a flourish of interest from the public gallery.

A brief pause ensued and the Judge removed his glasses and gave me a stern look. The defence and prosecution Barristers both glanced at me with a look of wonder and bowed their heads in silent anticipation of what I may have understood by their question. I really had no idea what he had meant when he asked if I understood. By now all eyes were on me, and even the accused in the Dock looked on and said something barely audible to me along the lines of, 'It's you.' I could feel myself blush bright red and sit upright and rigid, preparing for the next blow of the court. I was quite bamboozled by the events of that moment. Could it be that I really had no idea what I had been called to the court for?

The Judge called for the court to start by asking the accused to identify himself, which he did, all the while looking straight ahead. I looked down upon him, feeling all-powerful and important. The Jury sat, looking tired, and the public gallery all looked on with smiles on their faces, all sure they would be right in their judgement. The Barristers and court staff sat down, preparing their notes so they might start their deliberations.

The Judge then called for the prosecution to take the stand, and the elderly QC, with his wig and cloak, stood tall amongst the smaller figures in the courtroom and started to present his case by remonstrating the evidence against him.

The court continued for a further 10 hours. It sat from 9am till 7pm. By the time I left I was exhausted and settled to stop at a nearby bar, The Grosvenor, to have an under-age drink and a cigarette. I thought back to the day I had just had. There would be a further week of this deliberation, maybe more, and I was unsure of what I was witnessing. Furthermore, I had been quite shaken by the whole topic of murder within the court, as I had only ever read about it in the past. Now I was sitting in court, party to the conviction of a double murder. As I say, I was shaken by the events of that day and began to think that maybe I knew something about the case.

Just maybe I had witnessed this murder take place. I was certain my mind was playing tricks on me, and my conscience had not spoken to me yet, but something was turning the cogs of my subconscious and revealing a terrifying image of a child running down a street brandishing a shotgun. I dismissed it as paranoid and settled to leave the bar behind and return home to the love of my family.

My mother was in the kitchen making a lasagne for dinner when I arrived home at 8pm. I immediately began to tell her about my day in court and what I had witnessed in my new vocation as a student of law. As you could have guessed, she was very proud of me at this moment in my life. I was her darling, and I could do nothing wrong. And as I related my tale of the accused's indictment she smiled throughout, thinking I was her wonderful boy, sure to make a success of my life.

The reality, however, was soon called into question that very same day. Having spoken to my mother at length, assuring her she could be proud of me, I stepped outside to call on the one and only friend I saw regularly in those days, Paul Bennett.

Paul, as usual, was to be found standing at the entrance to his mother's drive, drinking strong beer. He was a couple of years older than me, and I was always looking up to him as a role model on how to be a man; he was my closest buddy. I greeted him the same way I had always done, with a cheer of victory and a punch to the air, and as always he handed me a beer without me having to ask.

So there the two of us stood, in the darkening light of a late summer afternoon, 9pm in my home town, talking about my inspiring and gloriously successful new venture into the world of law. I had made some sacrifices to get this far though. Before I had made the choice to follow the path of a student of law, I had played in Paul's band, The Rag Time Kunts, with his brother Trevor, and his nephew Martin Partington. Paul himself was also having some success in his chosen career as a musician, after enrolling at college to become a sound engineer. The two of us were both very proud of ourselves, and our mothers would watch from their front room windows, keeping check on their two favourite sons.

We talked about our current plans while keeping tight lipped about what future we may like to create for ourselves. I happened to mention at the time my old girlfriend I had been seeing some months previously when Paul, with his one of his usual flashes of brilliance, raised his finger to stop me in mid flow and nipped off back to the house to attend to something relating to my topic of conversation.

When he returned, he brought with him a lump of cannabis and handed it to me. I looked at it, wondering what he had in mind. After all, I was well on my way to becoming a legal beagle and I wanted none of the life I had left behind a few months earlier when I had left Simeon by the wayside, to become a successful student of law. It was true it had only been about two weeks since I had decided I would no longer smoke, but Paul was insistent that I should build a spliff and relax. After all, I was no longer in court. I was reluctant to agree, and stood firm in my conviction that drugs would not help me achieve my ambition of becoming a Barrister one day. Paul simply shook his head and told me to forget it, before asking me if I would like another beer.

'Yeah,' I said.

Paul turned away from me and showed his teeth, then crushed his can in his hands and turned on his heels away from me to go fetch another couple of beers. I remained outside, waiting.

I waited for ages; at least half an hour or more in the rapidly falling temperature, until I got fed up of standing alone outside. As the rain began to fall I took off in the direction of home to settle into a sleepless night of hostility.

The day that followed was long and boring. The prosecution went about disseminating its evidence to the court; a shotgun, a long duffel coat and pictures of the dead men's bodies taken by the forensic team at the site of the murders. The QC then went on to bring expert witnesses to the bench to testify the science behind each piece of evidence. Many of them I thought I recognised. The expert witness who testified that the shotgun presented to the court was the same one that shot the cartridges that were found at the scene of the crime, looked so similar to my form tutor from school that I had to dismiss my thoughts as coincidence, and I continued to pop mint imperials into my mouth to alleviate the boredom.

By twelve noon, the court was dismissed for lunch and when I returned, I was turned away by the defence Barrister who told me the court was being closed for the rest of the day because a member of the jury had been taken ill. I asked if there was anything else I could be getting on with. He simply told me to go home and get some rest because tomorrow would be a big day. Feeling my enthusiasm was failing me, I set off back into town to catch the bus home.

On my return, I found the house empty. My mother would be at work, I assumed, and I settled down to make something to eat. I was about to switch the TV on for the duration of the afternoon, when my friend Simeon, whom I hadn't seen for weeks – ever since I said I would be working in the courts – pulled up outside in his car and moved down the path to the front door at speed.

I answered before he had a chance to knock, and greeted him with a wave of the hand.

'All right!' he said.

'Yeah, I just got in…' I replied.

He asked me what I was doing that afternoon.

'I was just going to stay in and read some of the legal books' I told him.

'No, you're not!' he assured me.

'Why, what's up?'

'Come out' he said.

Without thinking, I finished my sandwich and stepped out into the street, following him up the path to his car. Paul was standing on his mother's drive, as usual. I waved him over, but he ignored me and turned his back on me before withdrawing back into his house. I sat in the passenger seat of Simeon's motor, and we took off down to his flat on the far side of town where I had left him a few weeks previously.

Simeon was a hard man. Not a sharp and dapper person, he was scruffy and unkempt and often had a faint whiff of Caerphilly about him in later years. A man of many depths of feeling and often controlling in his behaviour, I admired and respected him for his trusted friendship. He always had my back in any eventuality. Unfortunately, he also buggered me in this position often enough to make my arse fall out of my pants before I was 18. So I guess he liked me just as much. It was a shame I couldn't trust him; really, I couldn't!

We reached his flat before the clock struck 5pm, ate Chicken Supreme from a tin and set off out for the night. First stop - Howies, on the corner of Station Road. He came raging out of the house like an old hippy who had done too much acid and threw himself into the front passenger seat of the car, where I was sitting. He quickly tired of explaining that I was in his seat and began pushing me through the gap in the chairs to the back seat of the car, all the while shouting and hollering that I was gay and could go and get fucked. After much kicking and fighting I eventually found my seat in the rear, only for a tap at the window to call me to open the rear door of the saloon to let his girlfriend and future mother to his children, Laura, into the car. I budged over, sitting behind Simeon now, and prepared for take-off.

As soon as we got started, going up the road to our first deal of the night, the talk was about acid. Or should I say 'E'. Howie had managed to do a deal with some African witchdoctor; an ounce of good weed for 50 pills.

At a tenner a push, they were sure to be in top demand at our intended destination, the Waverton Barn Party. But before we reached there, there was money to be made.

We travelled around town for about an hour and a half, criss-crossing the neighbourhoods and stopping at the houses of all his known friends. All kinds of smoking, laughter and love buzzes were exchanged in the smiling faces of all those who appeared at their doors as we called. Money changed hands, and soon we were on the home straight, so Simeon could have a shave and a shit. Before we could reach home though, we had an unfortunate incident.

A car pulled out in front of us, cutting us up, and Simeon called the chase. In pursuit of the car ahead, I could see 5 heads all on the bounce turning and looking at us with greedy stares of violent intent. We chased them as far as the car wash, even pulling up alongside them chanting hate and violence, when the cruiser that patrolled our streets appeared on the other side of the road. We didn't stop. We went for the lights, we jumped the clear red signal and took off along Stanney Lane, scuppering the fight for just one night. Shocked and scared by what had just happened, I asked why Simeon and Howie wanted to give chase. Simeon turned his aggression on me;-

'He's going to fuck you...!' he screamed in my ear, so loud my anus went into a spasm.

'Yeah, you fucking queer!' cried Howie. 'He Is.'

I assumed they meant someone in the car. I was about to say that it was him, Simeon, who had buggered me the week previous to my 13th birthday, but he shut me up with a short and intimidating rant on how I had to grow up and be a man, like him. Perish the thought! I shut up and turned my head to hide the tears a 15 year old would shed. Soon we were back at Simeon's, winding up the beginning of a great night out, in spite of the injustice I had faced and the threat of further attacks in the future.

By 10 pm, the party at the barn dance was swinging. Everyone from the area had arrived and the DJ's did set after set of banging house tunes. Not that this was to my taste, but it did go well with the ecstasy I had taken before leaving Simeon's. My first pill produced a kaleidoscopic cornucopia of trembling emotions, religious fervour and extreme bubbling highs that I had never thought I could experience, not in this life anyway. Gradually I got to meet people. I was introduced to several key players in my high school drugs supply, including Ming and his second partner other than his wife, Robin. I had known of Ming from an earlier incarnation of my life as a dope fiend. He lived nearby and was well known as a major player in the trade. Until now I had memorized his image into my minds eye as the dangerous one amongst us. The lone wolf. Here though, he was animated and jovial about his career as a coke dealer. He had no shred of concern for some time spent in jail. He had lived and learned it before.

We talked on at the entrance to the rave. Ming told me he was trying to corner a market in coke by selling to some of my friends from school. Afraid of the demon drug cocaine, I shied away from all his attempts to involve me in the distribution of his product and half stumbled, half fell across the room to the wall on the far side of the barn and collapsed in a heap on the wooden boards to the crash of distorted hardcore ripping into the PA.

Suddenly I was confronted with Ming's new supposed girlfriend, Robin. A strange name for a girl, I know, but Rob, as we affectionately knew her, was a looker back then... A startling face for a girl, her eyes glittered like diamonds with a clear youthful expression that would launch a thousand ships. Her pale rose lips and a slim figure suggested she would give nothing away about her intentions, and she was truly devoted to Ming as I would discover for myself many years later. Right here, right now however, she seemed too attractive an opportunity to turn down.

I jumped to my feet and caught hold of her outstretched arm, pulling her down towards me. I was excited under the influence of this new fangled drug and saw sense in proving my masculinity. I drew her waist closer to my groin as I slowly stood and held her firmly in my stare. I went to kiss her... and Ming dragged her away from me. On the far side of the room behind them Simeon was looking right over, smiling and making hollering whoop, whoop noises.

'Aehhhh, Shane! Rob, eh?' He was falling about the place laughing, high on ecstasy, his eyes glazed and rolling in his head.

I gathered myself together and set off for a trip across the sparse room towards the mingling happy people on the other side. As I set off, a lace had come undone on my shoe and as I took the next few unsteady steps towards my chosen target, I tripped and fell on my knees, falling forward and coming to rest lying face down next to Ming's training shoe. He instantly raised his foot and crushed my remaining dignity under the tread of his size 12 Adidas Samba.

A hand reached down and lifted me up from the floor. Simeon patted me on the back and welcomed me to his trusted circle of friends.

'Have her!' he cried in my ear.

'Who?' I asked, not knowing why I felt so good in this beautiful moment.

Ming took me to one side.

'Listen mate, you can have her all right. But you've got to sell for me.'

'I can't, I can't...' I protested. 'I don't know anyone who has got that kind of money...'

He explained to me the rules of the game he was inviting me to play. He sorts me the stash, I get the word out and then sit on it until people are crashing my door down.
I was interested for a moment; he said it so sweetly, like there was nothing wrong with the proposal he put to me.

'Your choice...' he said finally.

'Give me some time' I said, and brushed his welcoming arm away. 'I haven't even tried it yet...'

And with those words, my fate was sealed. From that day forward I was to become a member of Ming's gang. And my career in the courts was about to come collapsing down around my ears.

3. Nantyr

We met just after 7 pm, at Fergie's house in the centre of the city. The night had drawn in suddenly even though it was the middle of April, and the streets were littered with students from the university, plying themselves with cheap drinks from the many bars in the area. I knocked on the chipped and weather worn brown door and waited for an answer. Instantaneously, the dog began to bark. A ferocious rasp of a bark, more like a cough than a shout, and from the back room, I could hear Fergie pleading with the dog to keep quiet. It never did. Its incessant whooping bark continued until the door swung open and I was greeted by Fergie himself.

'All right Shane! – Come in, come in!'

Fergie's hello's always made me feel welcome here. In spite of the junk and clutter than filled every room, I loved this family more than most. They were virtually my own, and even though I no longer lived here, it always felt like I had come home to those that I loved.

We were the typical family, I thought. We all shared the same belief that love was thicker than finances and lived in each other's pockets, if not in our beds. It was certainly the perspective I had, even if the truth was far different. OK, we didn't always see eye to eye, but if I was ever in need of food, a drink or a bed for the night, then I could always call here.

Fergie showed me the way through to the back room. As I passed the front room I peered in at my aunt and cousin, sitting in front of the computer. They called out their greetings and I waved back at them from the hallway. In the back room and kitchen, Fergie had already prepared the night's supplies of cider, ham sandwiches and cigarettes all in a flight bag, that must have weighed as much as me.

'We all clear then, for tonight?' I asked.

'Yeah, yeah, I'm just waiting for Sam to call. He's going to show us the way up.'

Already the adrenaline was pumping, and I wasn't sure whether this night was going to be a success.

I had only met Fergie's wild friends a few times before and wasn't sure I would ever consider them friends of mine. They were all right, I suppose. Maybe a bit antsy towards me, and they were all of a criminal fraternity, but that didn't faze me. I had smoked for years now and had rubbed shoulders with much tougher people than the Spiral Tribe. At least so I thought.

Fergie continued rushing about, tending to the wife, my aunt, and gathering together torches and firelighters and such; anything we may need for the ensuing journey into Nantyr, where tonight I was invited to a gathering.

I was unsure of what to expect. It had been a long time since I had shown my face in a public bar and an even longer time since I had been to a festival. The last one I remembered going to was Creamfields, in the September of 1999, when I had flunked out of college.

The particular reason I had been invited to this gathering in the woods of Nantyr, was I had turned 24 that month and tonight's journey was a birthday treat.

The phone rang and Fergie spoke to Sam. Fergie handed the phone to me. Sam tried to give me directions to his flat in the suburbs of town, but I had no idea where on earth we were supposed to meet and so it was decided that Sam should meet us at Fergie's place.

'We'll pull up outside, be ready…' he told me.

I put the handset down and sighed in anticipation of what kind of night it was going to be. It could be the worst or the best night of my life so far, and I had not had time to check on my star signs that day to see what the evening might bring.

'You all right, Shane?' asked Fergie.

'Yeah, just a bit nervous…'

And I was! The anxiety lifted me from my usual cabbage like state, sprawled across the couch, cowering from the dissenting voices of those who did not share my vision, and took me to new highs. I felt fully conscious for once in my life, and after years of complaining that I was being treated unfairly because of my mental illness, I was choosing to rise above the petty vindictiveness I held in my heart for those I shared my life with and go to this party.

Fergie handed me the bag containing the crates of cider for the evening and I set out the door to the car and placed it in the boot. Behind me Fergie raced across the road in front of oncoming traffic and chucked the coats in the back seat of the car, then joined me, shotgun, in the front were I was waiting patiently for the arrival of Sam.

A few minutes later, he did arrive in his grandfather's car. He and his partner, Steph, pulled up alongside and spoke to Fergie through the open window. We were to follow them to Denbigh, then follow the directions up the mountain to the country park where the party was going on. Having organised the wagon trail, we hit the road.

Soon we were creeping up to a steady 70mph on the by-pass, right behind Sam and Steph. The horizon of Wales loomed into view through the darkness and before long we had made a right turn towards Denbigh and had got lost. We travelled as far as we dared into unknown territory before we turned around and parked up near the foot of a hill and consulted the directions given to Fergie by text message. As for myself, I had no idea where we were and we all seemed to be relying on each other. I waited in the car while Sam 'the man' and Fergie turned to a map to consider our next moves. They talked with one another for a time and then we set off to climb the hill above us, into the mountains of Nantyr.

The winding track took us up through the narrow lanes of the village and out towards the wild heartlands of Wales.

'Sheep, sheep everywhere. Mutton daggers at the ready and a bowl of mint sauce.'

The Macc Lads song resonated through the stereo. Fergie told me to stop what I was thinking, with a great display of hands and curse words. I cooled my enjoyment and played along, hoping this night would make up for the years I had been kept out of all the social events in my friends' lives.

By the time we arrived at our destination, a logging forest at the top of a ravine, we were all psyched up and ready to go. We pulled up at the side of the dirt track in front of a line of maybe 50 cars. We exited our vehicles and set off down the slope that led to the entrance. Through the pine forest I could see lights ablaze inside multicoloured domes. Had anyone passed by this way en route to some other destination, they would have assumed a spaceship had landed and the aliens had arrived.

We trudged on down the path to the end, where we were stopped by a young lad sitting in the passenger seat of a van. Fergie immediately flew into full blown chatter with him and introduced me to his friend, Dale.

Dale looked me over from the warmth of the cabin and commented on my dress sense. He said I looked very smart, and was the best dressed. Sure, he was toying with me as I was wearing Red jeans and a hoodie by George, but I was flattered, thinking I had made the most effort to attend.

Fergie and Dale talked for a moment and then asked,

'Have you been to one of these before?'

'No.' Pure and sweet, I had not.

They laughed and exchanged comments on me with Steph, Sam 'the man' and Fergie. Then he offered us what everyone else had come for, MDMA.

'I've got some toffee as well.'

I declined the offer and swore to stick to cider and smokes for the party. My days of getting wasted were over for now, but I could still enjoy the rave.

Assorted, high people began to gather around the van, blinded by the psychotropic substances in their bloodstreams. I took a step back, not necessarily afraid but shaken by how wild the party seemed to be. It had been a long time since my youth. Briefly, I reflected on the earliest party I went to, back when I was 15.

Back then when I was a teenager I had been privileged to be part of the dance culture, but now I felt like a veteran. An elderly acid casualty, who had returned only to find his comrades all gone to seed after having families. At least I had Fergie here with me, he was a veteran of the 80's as I was of the 90's, but he had lived larger than me in the 90's in spite of his youngest daughter being born. I wasn't here alone.

We entered the party via a log that spanned across a ditch, to a clearing in the trees. The pungent aroma of skunk cannabis reached my nostrils immediately. I felt unsteady on my feet as the ground was uneven and sodden with rainwater and littered with branches dropped en route to the bonfire.

Gathered around the fire, an assortment of Sam the man's mates were huddled together to keep warm.

I reached them with a few slips and trips up an embankment and raised my hands to say hello. The crowd turned and looked down on me as I took my place near the fire. In turn, I looked on at the crowd gathered there, taking in their appearance and age; all younger than me. My racing pulse made me wonder if this night was such a good idea as my heartbeat became more pronounced. As I stood there, feeling out of sorts, I thought to myself of Hal Davis' lyrics to 'Anyone Who Had a Heart'… I swear I could hear it in the background of the pulsating bass rhythm as I looked downcast at the mud floor, raised on an embankment holding back a stream that flowed into the logging forest.

I looked up with a sharp sigh of anticipation. Surely, tonight was to be the defining moment in my life so far.

Again, I thought I could hear the chorus of the Burt Bacharach song. Then, abruptly, and with some feeling of scorn, the group I was with pushed at me, leaving me alone with just a can of beer for company. Feeling somewhat put out and down, I looked around me for my friends. All of them were leaving now, off towards their cooler friends in the darkness. I stood, solitary, looking around, my eyes pleading for my friends to come back and keep me company.

For a moment I was alone by the bonfire. I did a double take of my surroundings.

Above me, the road that brought us here led upwards towards the mountaintop. In the gap between the trees, a Citroen Saxo shone its high beam down and across the pitch where the tents were placed, behind me. The two tents were crowded with late night revellers, all high on MDMA, and to my right was the logging forest, swathed in pitch black darkness. Finally, to my left, the group of friends I had come with were all closing in on me, talking in loud voices, with coarse words. My paranoid mind assumed they were talking about me, but the words themselves were inaudible. I was beginning to feel increasingly upset by the supposed words I could hear, and all of a sudden cried out loud...

'Leave... me... alone!'

I stood sobbing and waited for someone to comfort me.

I turned my face down again and considered whether anything that could have gone wrong, would have gone wrong by now. Steph, the girl of our group, arrived and stood next to me, holding in her hands a pack of tarot cards.

I greeted her presence with mumbled words. Next Fergie arrived and started dancing about to my right, hands in the air, jumping from one foot to the other. He shouted in my ear over the thumping beats, asking me if I liked Steph.

'Yeah,' I shouted back. I didn't have a better answer.

Fergie laughed and asked if I was gay. Not having a good enough answer to throw back at him, I called back;-

'…Yes Ferg… Of course I am.'

The crowd was gathered around us by now. All of the Ravers seemed to have crept out of the darkness and were standing, listening to our conversation.

To my left Steph took cards from the top of the pack, looking each of them over with an intense gaze.

'Damn!' I could hear her say.

I asked her if she had some bad news.

'No,' she replied. 'I think we got this wrong…'

Fergie continued to dance about from one foot to the other while I took in the sense of gravity I was now feeling. My heart sank as a hush fell over the crowd and the beats stopped.

The people stood to the sound of crunching snow underfoot…

'Suddenly…' the speakers announced.

'It's time for truncheon!' The crowd howled, laughing hysterically.

The insult went right over my head. I didn't know any of these people; even less, share any part of my life with them. I didn't realise they were being so cruel.

'Do you know the police?' Sam the man insisted on asking me.

'Yeah, I do…' It was true, I did know a copper or two.

'Fuck the police!' The crowd started shouting to the howl of whistles and chanting voices.

I looked to hide myself away but there was nowhere to go. I looked to Ferg, hoping he would come to my rescue. But he just danced about from one foot to the other, laughing at me from way out left.

Sam 'the man' turned to me and said…

'It's you, mate. That's why…'

My psychic antenna connected with his and he disappeared behind the crowd of girls that giggled amongst themselves. I recognised his sentiment and the message contained therein. A face was presented to me from out of the flames.

The stranger stared back at me from under his brow, turning his back on me and disappearing behind a crowd of girls.

Immediately, I began to hallucinate.

I could sense a feeling of heat behind me like someone's hand on my back. I turned and looked behind, looking for the person who was leaning on me. Nothing there...

Looking to my right and left. The crowd had drawn closer and was now gathered around the fire, with me. I looked at the dirt on the ground, feeling a sense of melancholy about my being here with all these strangers.

I chose to distract myself with thoughts about my then ex-girlfriend of sorts, Liz.

In a moment's breath, Fergie called out;

'Eh, Shane. Liz is here, you know?'

'No, Ferg. I didn't.' I called back.

At that moment I really wished he had not brought her here. I knew there and then that this relationship was about to be terminated.

Next, she appeared from nowhere, next to me.

'All right?' I asked.

She didn't speak. She just looked up at me, then turned away, staring into the burning embers of the fire.

I shrugged my shoulders and ignored her presence, except to exchange glances of contempt from left to right.

'Shane?' she queried me, '…well, it's like…' She sighed and rubbed her eyes.

'OK, I know! I know,' I said. 'It's over.'

'No.'

'I think it is, somehow' I snapped back at her. I wanted the final word, so I continued;

'You brought me out here with all these people to show me what I am. Didn't you?'

'Eh, Shane. Don't ignore her, whatever you do!' Fergie shouted out loud, laughing hysterically.

'I'm sorry Liz. I just don't love you.' I finally killed our precious romance.

'Who do you want to fuck then?' Dale called out from amongst the crowd.

'Go fuck yourselves!'

She smiled wryly, thanked me and took off in the direction of the entrance to the clearing.

'Eh, Shane. Well done Shane. At least you got her out of the way!' Fergie was literally falling over himself to my right, drunk out of his mind until he finally fell on my shoulder and said;

'You're right to fuck her off.'

My great evening was already falling apart about my feet. I sensed some presence behind me again, and, feeling threatened by the events, I turned and looked to see who was approaching.

Behind, I saw the face of an old friend, Simeon. Surprised by his presence, I greeted him with a cheer.

He slipped on in next to me and put his arm around my waist.

I wondered what was about to happen next. I asked him what he was doing here. I had not seen him in years. He just nodded down at me, looking stern. I felt weak and started sinking into the earth, only to have him hold me up.

By now I was finding this moment highly homoerotic, even though I was not explicitly homosexual. I smiled sweetly as he wrapped his arms around me, taking me in his embrace. I heard the sweeping sound of the wind through the trees and I raised myself to my full height to kiss him..., when he slipped away, unseen, just as he had arrived.

In an instant I was back at the party. The strangers that surrounded me were all laughing at me and I felt exposed, naked.

Looking down at my feet, all I could see was blackness. My coat, clothes, body were gone.

Liz appeared again.

This time she had taken on the appearance of the girl out of the Ting Tings, a pop group from the early part of the 21st century.

We talked briefly before Dale called out loud that the party should stop, waving his hands around in the air above his head. The music stopped and the crowd was silent.

Above, we could all hear the whoop-whoop of a police helicopter. It was circling us in the dark. A voice came over the tannoy telling us it was the police and we should stay still.

Before I could take all these confusing events in, Fergie launched himself at me and bundled me, half in blackness and through the flames of the fire, with a lot of force, into the river that flowed through the clearing.

In the clear, cold, fresh water of the mountain I felt stunned by all that was happening, like I had gone from sensory overload to sensory deprivation.

I lay in the water thinking I might be dead when I was lifted up from behind by a collection of the group gathered there. Out of the water that I lay face down in and back onto dry land, I breathed a sigh of relief. I was about to ask what on earth was happening when I was picked up and thrown back into the river again.

This time I lifted myself out of the water as the helicopter was moving away, the rumble of engine and propellers silently thumping the air above until the noise disappeared.

Drenched through, I staggered from the river to find Fergie.

In an intoxicated daze of alcohol and MDMA, the music started again and the lights of the tents became a porn star's studio and casting couch, but no girls were present.

Instead, all around gay men in tracksuits smelling strongly of semen wobbled back and forth through the throng of bodies, stopping by one another and offering to sell each other MDMA for a reduced price. One boy of about 17 stopped me, asking me if I was his dad and then assaulted me by throwing a punch which missed and sent him tumbling to the ground, before picking himself up like he was carrying a child and laughing hysterically. He then proceeded to run away in the direction of the bonfire.

I followed him…

…Dale was smiling at me from the other side of the fire. I stood on my haunches and shook with cold. My coat smoked as the heat steamed the moisture from the fabric.

'You're on fire, mate' Dale shouted across the heads of the watching crowd.

I looked up and tried to respond to his words but instead let out a whimper of a cry. I felt hurt, betrayed and humiliated. I went to approach him to ask him to protect me but he moved away, telling me to stay away.

The party was over.

Sam 'the man' came in close to me and got my attention.

'We need more wood for the fire.'

I was lead away to gather wood for the fire from a swampy puddle beneath the wooded area at the entrance to the clearing. I thought for a moment of a hexagram I had read in the I Ching. I remember the caption went, 'he shall wait in a place of blood, but will get out of the pit.' I was tired by now though, and chose to go get some sleep in the car.

I had found a new perspective.

'Terror.'

4. I am a Good Person.

I often try to tell myself that I am a good person, and it's not that I have doubts, but I am ashamed of the more perverse aspects of my personality. For a long time now I have believed I have a sick piece of work laying dormant inside me because my desires and history of indulgent sexual activity have made me afraid of the women in my life. Regretfully, I cannot love them as I should, not on an intimate, sexual level. I feel they are too forceful, too aggressive and far more able to express themselves sexually than I am. I feel my inbred, macho, masculine pride has been drowned in a sea of doubts and insecurities, fears and crying shame that nameless enemies may remark on as to my next moves. To be true, I am stuck here in this malaise of past guilty pleasures, shaken up by every person I meet on the street, who may recognise me as the crazy man who talks to himself.

This one particular morning I had not slept and was awake early at 8am. I had bathed, scrubbed my tar stained, blackened teeth and settled in front of my 3rd floor flat window, looking out across the street towards the children waiting for their bus to school. Winter had arrived by now. After a summer of showing off my pride in my new identity as a reliable, trustworthy and child friendly hero, I had finally succumbed to my fate to spend yet another year living alone in my one room, 3rd floor, terraced flat in the heart of another early industrial town in the north of England.

Just at that moment, out of the corner of my mind, a flutter of some miraculous creature came from the branches of the maple outside and perched on my window ledge. A robin red breast looked in at my world. My hand shakes as I wipe away a single tear caused by the acrid smoke of my rolling tobacco, reaching my eye: The same eye that spied the robin land. I see the robin turn his beak and spy back at me with the same feeling of worthlessness. I swear it shed a tear too. Then, with a flash of brown and red, it was gone again.

I look down upon the street. The children are gone and a tall woman stands in their place, focused intently on her mobile phone. Presumably sending a text. Then, as if she can feel my eyes gazing down at her, she turns and looks over her shoulder and up at me, looking down upon her with feelings of melancholy. The one I lost, the one I shall find, the one I shall never meet? I ask myself. For sure, I know I will never find out... though I continue to tantalise myself with her presence until she boards the bus to town. As she does, I spy the Robin again, this time in the branches of the maple outside on the green. It looks both ways and disappears in a flourish of excitement, down towards the ground and away. It made me stop and think.

I had spent the year trying, with some success, to organise my thoughts into a sleek and seamless machine that people would look to with some feeling of pride in me. After all, I was finally doing something to better myself as a person by making all efforts to avoid temptation and control the power others exerted over me by way of coercion and influence. By the time the year was drawing to a close in November, I felt I had really succeeded in putting my early twenties and all the problems I had faced up to therein to one side and focused on a further, and, I thought, more attainable, goal; To return to my earliest childlike state, one of celibacy and lust for my mother. It would seem on reflection that in all my efforts to control how I felt about sex, sexuality and my preference, I had sabotaged my own libido for want of sanity and a clear conscience. But ultimately I had none of these valuable commodities. My values were as confused as my sexuality, and the only thing pronounced about me was my vanity.

The skies were blackened with the threat of later showers. The dim light that reached into my front room carried with it a shade of blue from the silver lining of the clouds. I thought it about time to turn in for the duration of the morning and afternoon. By now I was feeling so tired I had pins and needles in my face and arms, and every time I sat down I had to lie and rest a little. I closed the blinds and took to my feet, settling in under the cold linen sheets fully clothed. I lay there for a moment, just in stasis, thinking of nothing. A completely blank mind was presented to me. I pulled the sheets closer to my chin and said spontaneously, without considering the thought itself;

'Fuck off! Yer fuckin' nonce.'

Intrusive thoughts and mutterings had become part of my personality by now, and it was often put to me that I had an imaginary friend. These spontaneous urges to shout out profanities to the walls of the empty flat I inhabited had baffled my neighbours, I suspected, and had made me a reclusive and bitter man. Sometimes I felt my only friend was my psychiatrist. It wasn't that I did not have a single friend I could trust with what I said. It just felt better to share my problems with her, instead of someone who potentially would use the conversation as gossip. Sometimes I felt I couldn't even trust her, and doubted the confidentiality of our discussions. I realised, however, that I was largely to blame for the stir I had caused by writing a blog exploring my feelings toward the people I was obliged to involve myself in on a daily basis. Crucial to the inspiring thoughts preoccupying my mind were my feelings toward the children I knew and saw each day. And that is where the trouble starts.

I woke again at 2.46pm and stumbled into the kitchen to make a brew. My mouth was sour with the morning's accumulated floss of 30 cigarettes, washed down with litres of tea. I poured out the kettle, spilling the contents over the already tea stained sideboard. I swished the teabag round and cleared up the mess with a soaking tea towel impregnated with the odour of sour milk and stale breath. Stepping into the front room, I raised the blinds half way and peered out onto the bus shelter. Sitting down, I switched on the TV and immediately turned to ITV3, to watch the later edition of The Jeremy Kyle Show. I turned to look at the weather, noticing the splash of raindrops on the puddle in the road and felt the chill of the cutting wind rushing through the branches of the weeping maple. I lifted my mug and took a big, deep slug of my tea and rolled a cigarette. My day had started as any other, late and without meaning.

The show on TV pricked my conscience about my past with my ex-partner. As every other couple from a town much like my own, we would fight over the paternity of the children who by rights should never have been born to a bullshit emotion such as love. Contraception was the name of the game, and I felt someone wasn't telling the whole truth: Like I had been misled by that textbook of Freud's, explaining the reproductive cycle to boys younger than myself.

By the time I had finished smoking my first cigarette of the afternoon and lit a second, I was running low on papers and got to my feet to go fetch another packet from the shop. I put on my coat and left for the front door.

The journey to the shop was a short trip around the corner of the tenement block I lived in, to Thelwall Road, where a row of shops including a sandwich bar, chippie and solarium, as well as the mini mart I was going to be visiting, were situated.

I stepped through the double doors and into the warmth of the store. Immediately on entering, there was some excitement at the till. One of the women who worked there was laughing and shouting out loud at the sight of a bird, making a nest for itself in the loft space, above the polystyrene tiles that made up the ceiling. I ignored the commotion as I searched for change at the back of the store, seeing if I could afford a pint of milk. Behind me the robin I had seen earlier skipped between the aisles, from one shelf to another, much to the amusement of the small children gathered around the front of the store. Having counted my change, I took a pint of milk from the shelf and turned towards the aisle where the primary school kids were gathered, and stood amongst them, waiting to be served.

The queue soon dispersed leaving just the 3 children, some woman, the shop assistants and me at the till.

'All right,' I said, 'err... can I have a packet of Rizlas too?'

'Yes, love... ' The woman behind the counter smiled, pointed down at one of children waiting and said that it's good luck to have a birdie in the shop.

'Is it?' the little dark haired girl asked.

I looked around to see the robin skipping about on the floor. Behind me the same tall woman I had seen earlier that morning, at the bus stop, was standing with a small child of her own. Dressed in a bobble hat and pink coat, she was looking on in amazement at the sight of the little birdie jumping about amidst her feet, singing its sweetest tune.

'There's a little birdie in here, is there?' I said to her.

'Oi, don't talk to her...' the shop assistant called.

The smallest girl popped her head from around the back of her mum's legs, all the while clutching her thigh and answered...

'Yeah!'

The shop assistant sighed with expectation.

'And don't you be mean, you!' the woman scolded at the other girl.

I thought to tease her a little.

'He'll be talking about you.'

'Will heee?'

'Yeah! Birdies talk, don't they?' I asked the woman behind the counter, hoping she would enjoy the tease just as much as me.

'Yes, they do...' she said very abruptly.

The little one stood aghast in anticipation of what else the birdies might have said.

'Is he right?' the second of the pair asked.

The blonde shop assistant leaned over the counter and struck out at her with a defiant

'No! It's not for you.' The little girl looked glum.

I continued...

'It's all true, they did you know...'

'Birdies don't talk!' the little one shouted back at me, cross at being teased.

'Ahh, but they do. If you get up early in the morning you can hear them talking.'

'Do they?' she asked with shortness of breath. Her imagination was being brought to the fore by now, and she looked on at the robin flitting from shelf to perch, her eyes ablaze with wonder.

From the middle aisle, a third girl, in her early teens, poked her head around the corner to add her tuppence to the conversation.

'You're not our dad!'

I ignored her wit and answered back.

'I could be your boyfriend though.'

She stopped what she was doing by the teabags and called out...

'Nooooo, nonnnnccceee's... here!'

'Yeah that's right' I said. 'You're not too old for birdies either...'

'Gary is' the shop assistant told me. Then shrugged her shoulders and laughed.

'Is he?' I wondered to myself.

'Yes. What do you think?' she asked.

'It's the stuff dreams are made of, that's what I think...'

The mother in the long duffel coat laughed with her hand to her mouth. Hardly containing her amusement at the look of the children all standing there, with expressions of absolute glee, she said:

'Take her home if you want...'

'...Yeah,' I said. And after a pause to think, continued: 'I think I would like that!'

Laughing, I turned back to the shop assistant and placed my milk and the Rizlas in a bag.

'You're sure...?' the shop assistant began to tease me.

'Yeah. She should have been mine, that one...'

The shop assistant looked me over with a surprised smile. The children gathered there all looked to me with blank expressions of wonder.

'Is he my dad?' the little one asked.

'No...' the blonde shop assistant replied, smiling.

The other shop assistant finished buttering scones and told me to stop teasing the kids.

'Is he gay?' the little dark haired girl asked.

'Yes, I think so...' the brunette assistant said.

The teenager of the group was hiding behind the shelves of the middle aisle by now, laughing hysterically to herself. Amused by the cheek of it all, I thought to spare myself any further blushes.

'All right, I'm going now anyway. Ta ta, you...' I waved to the lovely little one I had teased with talk of birdies. The teenager and the third girl then ran to the back of the shop to give chase to the robin, shouting obscene words about me as they did.

Then, as I opened the door to leave, the robin leapt from the shelf behind the door and flew out into the street, brushing over my shoulder so I could feel the soft feathers on my cheek, and away. Without realising the magic that had just occurred, I stepped away from the shop front, homeward bound to make myself a brew.

I settled into the afternoon with a cup of tea and a chain of cigarettes. Outside in the street, the little lover I had seen in the shop was waiting with her mum for the next bus to town. I gazed down upon them with happy eyes as my little lover ran back and forth with her friend, playing with a tennis ball. The thought occurred to me that she may have been one of my own children, the result of some previous drunken occasion involving a pig and a poke. Sure, it was unlikely as I didn't recognise her mother, but then, she could always have been adopted...

And there, in the branches of the late green maple tree, the birdie was looking down upon her, singing his sweetest song and flashing his red breast to the sky.

Just then, from way out left, the teenager appeared from out of my line of vision and ran down the path to the tenement building I resided in. The buzzer rang out and I went to the hall and raised the receiver to my ear.

'Da,' she said. 'Can I come up?'

5. The Ackers Household

Chloe heard the door go, but didn't get up from the floor where she was playing her X Box. The stranger entered the room with a scent of something green on the breeze. He looked down at where she sat playing her console and lifted his boot to step right over her head, when her mother called for her to move quick, and let the man pass. She shuffled on her bum across the wooden flooring, out of the path of the tall man, who was unshaven and dressed in khaki colours. Howie, her dad, popped his head around the kitchen door frame and called out to the man in a taunting manner but with good feeling;

'Ahhh, here's the little fucker!'

'Yeah Howie, how yer doing?' The strange man was in the kitchen now, out of sight.

'Where did you get to then?' she could hear her father asking.

She could hear a closed conversation taking place behind the wall that separated the front room and the kitchen. She didn't recognise the man, but his voice was familiar, and as the man spoke to her father, her mother called out to her older sister upstairs.

'Kim! Someone's here...'

Downstairs, Kim could hear the voice of her father throwing taunting insults at the visitor in good humour. She knew her dad; he was the kind of father that didn't care a great deal about the day to day concerns of the family, but he could be relied upon to hold his ground when his family were in a fix. Right now she could hear her dad talking to her mother, Lauren, about her. Thinking she might be missing something, she left her bedroom and called down the stairs to her mother, asking who the visitor was.

She didn't answer, except to shout back that she should come downstairs. In a minute, she was down the apples and pears and standing in the front room facing her mum, asking who had arrived.

'That man's here' Chloe told her.

'Who? What man?'

'Take a look' said her mum.

Kim took a peek around the corner of the door frame. A tall, sun kissed stranger stood in the kitchen talking to her father. She didn't recognise him.

'Who is he?' she begged her mum.

'Nellie. You remember him.'

She shook her head.

'You do,' she assured her, 'you used to like him.'

'He's a loon!' called her father, 'Aren't yer...'

'Yeah, Howie' the man said, obviously reluctant to give himself away, even to a child.

He looked upset or shaken by something. He flashed his eyes at her from behind her father and she retreated away to the comfort of her mother, on the couch.

In the kitchen, the conversation continued and money was exchanged. The man rolled a cigarette and the scent of wacky baccy began to pervade the air. Their father would often smoke the stuff at night, when they had all gone to bed. They both knew their parents used drugs, even though both Chloe and Kim knew it was wrong. Even Colin, the boy their father took around with him, smoked the stuff and he wasn't much older than them. Their dad even took coke, sometimes.

Howie called to Colin, who was sitting facing the computer on the leather back chair, to roll another cigarette. He immediately began putting papers together in a hurry, like he was going 'cold turkey.' The girls knew something about drugs. They messed you up because after a while, you couldn't do without them. They both couldn't wait to grow up and get started. Kim sniffed at the pungent aroma emanating from the kitchen.

'Stop that' Lauren told her.

'What?' Kim complained. Lauren shoved at her to get her attention.

'I wasn't doing anything' she whined.

'Getting high!' Howie said, laughing. 'And if you're finished with the computer, put it away.'

Lauren asked the girls to turn off their computer and watch the TV for a while. Chloe wanted to watch Beauty and the Beast, and Kim wanted to watch the cartoons. Lauren quickly tired of the bickering and told Chloe to put the DVD on. Kim skulked and threw herself back on the couch so hard she bounced right off and gave Chloe a kick from behind as she opened the DVD player. Chloe complained, while Kim chose her words. Lauren began to shout at the pair of them. At that moment, the man appeared from behind the door frame and announced he was leaving. Howie immediately began hurling his usual brand of comic insults.

'Arrhh, You're going fuck off now are yer?' Her father mimicked madness.

Oh, good! Shan't be seein' yer – I hope...'

'Yeah, that's right Howie, I'm going now.'

The man looked around the room at all the people gathered there; the girls, their parents and the boy – Colin.

'All right, Shane. Don't come back this time...' Lauren called. Howie laughed out loud and shoved the man to the door.

'And don't go writing anything about us either' she called after him.

The man, hunched over, slowly retired behind the door and could be heard to say he was sorry he had intruded into the life of the Ackers household. It was a sad moment. The man seemed very afraid of their father and unstable on his feet. Chloe asked if the man would be coming back.

'No,' Lauren replied, 'he won't.'

'I know him now,' Kim announced, 'is it him, who lived next door to us when I was little?'

'No,' Lauren told her. 'He lived with us.'

'Yeah.'

The girls looked at one another, and Lauren was satisfied she had solved all their questions about 'the man'.

Howie came from behind the door and raised his eyebrows at his placid wife.

'Looks like it's all sorted then' he said with a smile.

'Yep, I hope so.' Lauren looked up from where she was sitting. Howie was shaking his head with his hand to his brow.

'And don't ever, ever, come back!' he screamed out loud through the open window, as the stranger removed himself from the scene playing out.

Outside, I reached into my pocket and felt the £20 deal I had just purchased. I was on my way home to smoke it, but this day was one of the final indignities I had suffered. I had made my way back to the friends I was once with and taken in the bad feeling that lay between us. From here on in, life would be much simpler.

I have no idea why my youth was such a difficult time in my life. I could blame the older influences I clung to, the lack of care my parents showed me or my own rebelliousness. I don't know. What I do know is that my twenties were a very disturbed time. I was tired of the supposed lies I was obliged to live out on a daily basis, and my paranoid ideas about my childhood contributed to my state of mind as contained within this story.

Maybe this is what has upset me so much. I was taken from the street in the prime of my life and can never have the same opportunities I had back then.

I am not even allowed to pursue a relationship.

It's a pity because I have so much to give...

6. The Beast of F'iends

It was only when I reached 25 years of age that I gave a thought to my friendships. It appeared at first that I had a lot of trust invested in my friends and they, in turn, made excessive demands on my time and resources. I treated all of them with an attitude of jealousy and suspicion. Many times this worked to my distinct advantage. Not always though.

The three friends I had were Niggs, Martin and Alti.

Niggs, my Capricorn buddy, was a constant companion and source of many parallels of wisdom. Like him, I had a partner in my extended network of facebook friends. Someone I had not seen for many years.

During this period of my late twenties I had become more aware of myself and what made me happy. So upon reaching 29 I began to value the friendships I had invested my trust in during my formative years.

Niggs at the time was going through some kind of mid life crisis. His father was ill, diagnosed with Alzheimer's, while his elder brother was still suffering the effects of his experiences of the first Gulf War, some twenty years ago.

We were both in the late stages of our courtships with our childhood fiancées at the time of writing this down.

When push comes to shove and the odds are stacked against you, ready to fall and splice off the very achievement you treasure so much, then you realise how important it is to have a friend like Niggs, Martin or Alti, or any other. It is in these important relationships you will find an oasis of peace on earth.

We had a beautiful day on the river at Eastham. We travelled in a flash car at speed to our destination, had a drink or two each and a few cigarettes. We watched a motorboat cross the pier while planes came into land on the other bank, Liverpool John Lennon Airport. A huge bike with a 2.5 litre engine was parked in front of us, a Triumph I think. A great, huge beast of a bike. We sat on the wall overlooking the ferry and talked amongst ourselves.

Niggs couldn't wait to get what he had to say off his chest.

'Slags, sluts, sluuttss!'

'Niggs, you're terrible...' I replied.

'No! You say it all the time. Anyway Shag, you said you hate women.'

It was true, I had said it. I really didn't want to believe it though. After all, I had plans and had to deal with women every day, whether they be my mother, my aunt, my doctor or my partner.

But yes, they infuriated me.

7. Hello Starling (snow is gone).

A year earlier, the morning of 22nd of august 2004, I left the home of my aunt and uncle to get back to Egerton Street to bathe and eat. I spent a few minutes alone with just the TV for company watching Jeremy Kyle before leaving in the direction of Ming's.

The army barracks was on the outskirts of town and easily reached by means of a canal footpath. I arrived at about 11am to find Robin leaving for work. She asked me to look after the kids while she was away, leaving me to build my first joint of the day. Ming fell out of bed moments after Robin slammed closed the front door, and joined me downstairs on the couch.

Thumbing my arse up out of his seat, he threw himself down next to me and raised a fist in my face, as a symbolic gesture of defiance. I wondered who I had upset and sat there till late afternoon while Ming poked and prodded me, beating me in the chest and making some joke I didn't understand. I bombed more paste and chose to ignore his little joke.

By the time Robin returned from work I was feeling sick from the accumulated fur on my tongue from a whole day's smoking and was preparing to leave. Ming and Robin had their usual conversation behind the screen of the kitchen door, while the two children fought between themselves in front of the TV. Before the two of them could finish I announced I was leaving and stood to go. Robin called out for me to stay, as they had something important to say. I told her to tell me later and left for the road.

I stepped out through the red front door as I had done a hundred times and pressed on in the direction of home, along the bypass and towards the city. Darkness was closing in by now, earlier each evening, and I had to check the time. It was later than I had expected, 6.34pm, and it seemed I had not kept my hours. I put the time lapse down to the amount of speed I had taken that day and thought nothing of it.

I stopped at the railway bridge near Bache to watch the carriages pass. I was having palpitations and needed to stop to catch my breath. Having seen the train pass underneath I sat at the side of the road and rolled a cigarette. The traffic had slowed to a standstill except for a solitary police T5: that cruised past without even seeing me in the shadows. I felt weak, I felt beaten. I felt like I had something to fear. I felt the cloak of solitude wrap itself around me like a comforting embrace.

'I am done for,' I thought to myself, knowing I couldn't continue this way.

By the time I reached home and my bed, I was shaken by the intrusive ideas I harboured about what may come to pass in the meantime between my sleeping and present waking moment. I retired to bed just to lie there shaking with cold, afraid of all the demons that rattled around in my subconscious mind.

After several hours, I realised something was wrong and left my bed to walk slowly and surely under some marvellous and magical spell to the hospital A and E department. I had some trouble finding the doors to the waiting room as I had not been to that entrance before. Once inside I found there was no queue and I was attended to immediately. A female doctor made me sit a medical examination and asked what I thought was wrong. I told her I had a lot on my mind and was losing sleep over these supposed delusional images that constantly crossed my mind. That, and the foreboding feeling that all was not well. Somehow, I thought, this was the end. The sorry fate that should become me.

I was lead upstairs to a neat, clean bed and laid out to rest. A nurse came around and asked if I would like a wash or something to eat. I declined the offer and chose to just lie there with all these wonderful and weird images entering my mind.

During the night as I stared at the foot of the bedstead, a baby's cry rang out across the ward and nurses chattered amongst themselves with shrill voices. I peeped through the curtains drawn around me, trying to catch sight of the new mother in the bed opposite. Hours earlier it was occupied by an old man with tubes coming out of his nose and chest. He had gone now, in his place a new life... and at that moment the doctor arrived for the morning round. He drew back the curtains just a touch and looked down on me lying there frightened with a sneer of contempt for another drug casualty. At least that is what I saw. He let go of the curtain and let me be.

The nurse I had seen earlier in the morning arrived soon after and asked if I was OK. I asked if I could leave now and she said I was free to leave so long as I signed for a prescription. I agreed and gathered myself together, taking off my complimentary slippers and dragging my trainers from under the bed. I stood on legs too afraid and weak to run and drew back the curtain to catch sight of Hillary holding a newborn child in her arms. Before I could take it all in, and without a thought to the meaning of it all, she pulled back the curtain that had exposed her and hid herself from view. The nurse called me to the desk.

'Yes?'

'This is for you, Mr. Leah' she said, handing me my regular prescription.

'Thanks, I can go now, can't I?'

'You're free to leave at any time, Mr. Leah, yes...'

'OK, bye.'

'Byyyyyeeeeeeee...'

I walked away from the desk and the ward. It was around 6am and a very strong image had entered my mind of Jenna holding a playing card from the tarot deck, the 9 of cups.

The 9 of cups, the 9 of cups, the 9 of cups.

I focused on that thought as I strolled home to rest on my bed. The voices had been quiet at least, even if I was psychotic at this moment.

8. Blackmail.

I left the hospital gates around 6pm in the summer of 2002. I had come to be there after a serious bout of depression and anxiety caused by the breakdown of my relationship at the time of the millennium. It was not as though I had been there the whole time; no. Prior to my incarnation I had spent two months working at Rexham Plastics on the Deeside industrial estate, south west of my home town.

Tonight was just a temporary release from my chains. I had been discharged from Grosvenor Ward to return to my mother's house 10 miles away, in my home town. With no money in my pocket and no change of clothes, I could not take the train. Even if I bunked on at Bache, I would be recognised and thrown off by the first stop. Besides, I did not want to be seen making this journey.

The legal staff, who had been reading my notes for weeks were following me but I had no reason to fear them now. I was a free man. I decided to have some fun with them and so I took off along a green lane towards the canal until I was out of sight, and then disappeared into the countryside.

They would not find me until it was too late, even if I was the most hopelessly misguided fool.

As I trod purposefully along the byways of South Wirral I gave some thought to the reasons for getting incarcerated at the clinic. I had reckoned I had been wrongfully admitted at first. But as the doctor's questions became more and more unfeasible I had thought that maybe I was being blackmailed. By whom, I could not tell. But for sure, they were mistaken if they thought I knew what the matter was.

I reached my mother's house late in the evening. I was not supposed to be here as she had taken an injunction out on me just before I was sectioned following several ugly scenes between us in public. But I wanted to apologise. The sun was setting beneath a large cumulus cloud over the rooftop of The Princes pub and I was feeling surprisingly good about myself for having the courage to come here and say I was sorry. The street was unusually silent; not a soul in sight other than a stray dog that raced past, carrying some piece of litter in its mouth.

I knocked. No answer. I knocked louder and stood at the window, tapping at the pane of glass and peering inside, thinking that something was amiss. There was always someone at home, and it seemed to me as I cast an eye around the street that the place had been deserted. Suddenly, the door cracked open to reveal a man taller than me, with a small child at his feet.

Immediately he spoke to me as if he were expecting me to call.

'I'm sorry Shane, she doesn't live here any more.'

'No, you don't understand. I have come to see me mum...'

'I'm sorry. Try Whitby instead.'

'She's moved? How come? Do you know what number?

'No! Sorry. Now look, I have to let you go.'

I looked over his shoulder into the living room behind him. A child with blonde hair was standing in the kitchen doorway beyond with her jaw open, aghast. It was my alleged daughter. I put my foot in the door to stop him closing it in my face.

'Chloe! It's me, your dad! Tell your mother I'm here to see her.'

The kitchen door slammed shut and the man I assumed to be my ex's new partner shoved me back out the door.

'But..? She's supposed to be my daughter...!'

'I know. And I don't care!'

The door was slammed in my face. I turned around and faced the audience of neighbours that had gathered in their doorways up and down the street.

'What's up?'

One of them called to 'get out of here' as I skulked away from the scene of the disturbance and on to the nearest place I could think of; Simeon's.

I entered Simeon's like a dirty dog breaking and entering a bitch's back garden in summer: without knocking and announcing my arrival, I just let myself in and immediately confronted him with the news I had just been party to.

Hunkered down, he just gave me a grimacing look and turned away.

'Simi! Look at me... What the fuck is going on?'

'Shane...' he said, 'You're totally fucked...' He started to smile, then laugh out loud like he had hidden some terrifying secret from me.

I stood tall and thought of the reasons for his betrayal.

'...Is Robin dead?'

Simeon reached his right arm out and grasped hold of the handle of some object. I didn't know what it was. It was just a sharpened point on a handle.

'Sim!' I warned him. 'I need to know what's going on!'

He stared me in the eye with determination and cunning and suddenly threw his clenched hand at my heart. My heart stopped and I pulled his hand away from my chest, all the while holding tight to the weapon. He looked me again in the eye and then lowered himself, almost cowered down and went to turn away, waiting for me to drop.

With my left hand now I took hold of the weapon and plunged it 10, no maybe 20 times into his stomach and shoulder blades. I didn't stop for several minutes until he was silent: not breathing and still.

He didn't bleed straight away. But as I left the crime scene I stood in some dark sticky liquid seeping out from beneath the washing machine and where he lay. Stepping out on the wilton carpet in the hallway I exited from the front door and took off down the street. I could hear shouting from behind..., and strangely enough, cheering! I took a glance behind as I ran up the street, clutching my chest and weeping deliriously with joy and pain. Simeon was behind me, falling over himself to chase after me. He seemed unwounded and I stopped, certain I could finish this fight once and for all.

We faced each other several feet apart before he came at me with a flying kick. I fell down and was landed with several punches. Kicking and punching my way out of trouble, I got up and threw a head butt at him, only to bash my nose against his forehead so it broke and bled.

We stood apart for a moment, weighing each other up.

Simeon's second attack was less severe. He stood back, looking for the easiest knock-out blow. I could see in his eyes he was hoping to take some final victory uppercut at my jaw, and so I weaved the first blow. I dodged the second. I ducked down and I dived right at him and threw all of my anger into my left arm, cracking him clean in the right of his temple. He dropped.

Laying on the pavement, I could see he was wearing a knife-proof vest. The sound of ambulance sirens howled across town and I took off again in the direction of Whitby. As I ran I could see Martin walking down the street avoiding eye contact, and then took off in the opposite direction. By the end of the road the police were waiting for me.

I gave myself up. Placing my hands in cuffs and placing me with care in the back of the van, I knew I had finished with the trouble I had been dealing with for 5 years.

I had attributed my trouble as love. And from my perspective that was all I wanted to hear about. I had no thoughts of committing an evil act of betrayal, blackmail or rape. But how had brought all this upon myself...?

Back at the Princes' public house, Niggs, Martin, and Alti... all my friends, held court on what had happened to their friend. Niggs, presiding, alleged Shane had lost the plot and deserved a break.

'He's overworked!'

Simeon arrived at the same moment, shouting that Shane was going to serve time for his trouble. Howie stood proud behind him and said the unthinkable;

'He's a fiddler!'

Alti knew it was all bollocks.

'He's not going down!' he cried out loud.

At that moment a plain clothes policeman entered the bar, looking for trouble...

Immediately he reached for Niggs' collar and dragged him to the toilets. There was a huge commotion amongst the patrons. With Niggs blushing bright red and hollering for him to let go, he confronted him with the evidence. Pushing open the toilet window facing out onto a courtyard where no one could reach, he showed him the letters, scattered amongst the debris on the floor like torn pieces of litter.

'What's the deal, hey, mate?'

Niggs pretended he knew nothing about the circumstances of Shane's arrest and wrestled with the copper to break free. By now, the whole pub was standing in the entrance to the gents, watching and listening with disbelief.

'You must need your ears syringing...'

The copper dropped Niggs from up against the wall, leaving him sobbing on his knees.

'But, but..., but, I didn't know! It's Simeon, he's been paid to keep secrets from him...'

'Why?' The copper asked.

'So they can manipulate him... Otherwise he'll find out about Nell!'

Simeon pushed to the front of the crowd and relayed what had happened.

'He's not dead you know, Victor. That's why! If he ever found out he would go and find him. And the whole family's terrified of him.'

'Is this true?' the copper asked.

'Yes.'

'Damn!' ... It was all he could say.

Slowly the crowd dispersed and Niggs returned to his seat and his friends. Outside, Simeon was already leaving in his flash new car at speed, like a rocket ship to the moon. The day was done, and Shane was safe now. Even if some pride had been lost the family would continue to live, love and lose as they may. And Victor's legacy would forever remain a secret.

But I have to ask, why?

9. We Met At The Crying Steps

We met at The Crying Steps, outside the Old Orleans bar near the river. The five of us were drinking cider fetched from a bag, straight from the bottle. Soon we were to be joined by two others, a couple. They were to compliment our arrival by greeting us as friends before blazing off ahead of our little group, to have their romantic evening with just each other for company. So that left me, Fergie, my cousin Carmen, her boyfriend Kurt; and Steph, a family friend.

We were stood near the river in the midwinter cold, looking up at the walls of the City where we were to be joining the rest of the evening's visitors on tonight's excursion into town to enjoy The Chester Mystery Plays. Fergie jittered about making conversation with the group asking if they had ever been on a trip like this before. I had never been to one of these, unlike the rest of the group who had visited the Groves before to witness the creative endeavours of Chester's great and good. The tension and excitement in the air was enough to set my pulse racing and I was looking forward to something of an extra special treat.

We entered the gates from the foot of the walls, towering some hundred foot above the river and up the slight incline into the Groves itself, known as The Crying Steps. We were first greeted by an African woman handing out flyers about the events taking place that evening. I recognised her voice from a telephone psychic reading I had back in my early twenties. Considering that my secret may be out, I took her gift with caution and continued up the path.

The first turn in the path presented to us a woman playing a harp. Her words, amplified through a small speaker, resonated through the crowd gathered in a semi circle around the small mound of earth she was sat upon. I stood, hidden behind the rest of the group and listened to the tone of the strings, as she spoke of her experience of love and the power of dreams. I was remarkably and suddenly underwhelmed by her candid words and thought she must have some strong convictions on whomever she may have loved so much.

Fergie made a break for it and continued to make his way further up the hill, chasing after his daughter with me straggling behind, whilst drinking Carling from a tin.

All around were unusual sounds and smells: Bongo drums, bells, rattling tambourines; the scent of lavender and camomile. Spices, aftershave, the pungent aroma of cannabis and the stench of leaf litter. Lights flickered and played upon the walls of the city and lasers mapped out the reaches of the horizon from the north to the south as we reached the top of the second display.

Round a hedge and through the next turn in the road we came upon the ending of a performance play and the beginning of the next chapter. One of the two actors called out to the crowd for volunteers to join them in their short performance and I pushed Fergie and Carmen to the front, offering them up as a sacrifice. The male of the two actors did a head count of our group and I found myself leading them out onto the green to take part in some sort of play. The story however, was yet to make itself known to me.

The female of the group talked on her microphone about the values of Fibonacci numbers and their associated meanings to Roman Chester. The male measured the distance between us and suggested we take a step forward or backwards depending on what number we were assigned. We were then offered a large corrugated plastic brick each and asked to place it in front of us. These were the stage props of the play. They represented separation and solitude.

'Do you feel a draft, Shane?' Fergie asked of me.

Carmen was stood in front of me.

'No, I'm quite warm, actually.' I said.

Fergie laughed and started fraternising with the assorted strangers who had joined us at the headcount to represent the wall.

Next, the male of the two actors made his way up the line of us extras to talk to each of us in turn. When he reached me his studied my hands. He turned them over and stretched my fingers along the length of his palm before asking me if I took part in any sports.

'No, I answered.

'OK.' He said. 'I must be wrong.'

Fergie then asked what he had said to me. I repeated the actors words and suggested he should have realised it was the cigarettes and alcohol that had made me.

The crowd looked on somewhat unimpressed by my efforts to make them laugh so I tried harder.

'That and the drugs, sex and pornography…'

'EH! Shane, no!' Fergie was talking animatedly to me now saying no one found that funny.

In front of me the crowd gathered there were cast in shadow and I could not see their eyes looking back at me, though one – and I assume it was a woman, flashed her teeth at us like the flashbulb of an old camera, her smile blazing through at Fergie's antics behind me.

Carmen asked when she could leave.

'Now if you like.' Said the male actor.

And so we placed our plastic blocks on the ground and left the arena to join the crowd. All except Fergie, who clung on to his plastic block and asked to take it home as a souvenir. After a short exchange of words, he left it behind and we ran off around the green.

Here, I encountered quite a surprise, as a woman I recognised as Jenna was weaving a web of red wool around some steel structure between some benches. I greeted her sincerely, not with token emotion but with respect for an old friend and taking the wool from her I wove a thong shape between the branches of a weeping willow and the park bench, before handing the reminder of the wool to back to her and chasing off after Fergie and the gang, who it seemed, didn't want to be shown up by me any further.

Up, up and up the hill and into an open square that displayed a Roman hypocaust, we met with a short drama between two roman deities. The god's of wine, women and song: fury, war and weather. Together they skirmished over the death of their shared wife, Mother Earth. The two of them, clad in tunics and sporting their weapons of battle took turns to lay the other down. The first god, drunk himself into a stupor with red wine, before scraping the strings on his lyre, and then dying through ingesting hemlock. The other threw lightening bolts, pails of water and ran the first god through with a sword as he met with his last dying breath and seeing his folly had some vanity to it, had worn himself out and fell asleep.

It was something of a wild performance but before I could make sense of the play, Fergie and the group were moving on past a woman dressed as an old hag with the latex nose and 18th century costume, selling vials of 'real tears' from an old trunk and trying hard to make a sale of any of the woes she had collected, and I went after them to the exit of the Groves. Here, a woman I recognised from my home town read out, blow by blow, the history of catastrophe within Western Europe from the dawn of the Roman Empire to the present day, making particular reference to the global conflicts of the twentieth century. The finally, we were ushered quietly and quickly out of the gates and onto the street.

But that was not to be the last of this experience. So far it was an assault on the senses; a psychedelic trip of light, sound, drama, film and the history of catastrophe, and up the stairs to the sandstone gateway it ended, with a brief flicker of starlight from above the road on Eastgate, where an astronomer trained his telescope upon the Dogstar: Sirus B.

Each of us was handed an A4 piece of paper that had some scrapbook story typed upon it about the end of Chester City and of the Universe, but it was rolled up so as to make a cone that I used to train my eye on the flashing red star in the east of the sky. It was just left and to the top of a distant constellation, much like Orion and his Belt - that I may have thought was much larger, usually, this time of year. In my memory it would fill the sky during November...

And then, home. There was nothing more to see that evening and we wandered aimlessly like we were lost in a narcotic dream of each other through the city streets, passed the drunks and homeless of Chester, the real people of the old town, and the towering monotheist spiritual home of those who had lost their love for want of a quick fix or a fresh pound of flesh.

The sky was still circling above and I could still see the flashing red pulse of the Dog Star beaming its warning down upon us. 'Do Not Come Here,' it seemed to say. I turned to Fergie in a moment of inspiration and let him know what I was thinking...

Fergie looked up at the sky and turned to me an said,

'What makes you say that Shane? It's not a star, that, it's a plane or something. Isn't it?'

Carmen added I was crazy or high and I should stop listening to, 'That Jewish Guy.'

I consoled myself with thoughts of my own pride and was about to make a case for why astrology was such a brilliant tool for adding depth to a persons' life, when, poof! The fireworks display started behind us, red flashes of glitter and gold cascaded down upon the roofs of the ancient city and I soon forgot about the myth of the Dog Star and we hurried to make our way home.

Carmen asked her father, whether her mother would be home yet?

'She should be. Depends on whether she's finished...'

'Why's she working so late?' I asked Fergie.

Fergie answered back that she wasn't.

Fergie opened the battered and beaten down door and we rushed inside huddled together as a litter of kittens may do when born in a barn, when Barb appeared from the kitchen, asking if we enjoyed our trip and whether we would like something to eat? I cast a look at her from behind Steph, thinking all the time of the woman we encountered at the Groves playing the harp and the similarity of their appearance.

Barb smiled and took our requests for cheese on toast and tea, and then went back to her work...

...Outside in the street, people went about their business as they had done throughout my life. My adolescence was spoken for and my innocence lost. I thought about fate and how only that could change the future now, I had done all I could to find happiness. The special people, friendly faces and offers of support were here. There was nothing more I could ask for...